Finders Keepers

PG Forte

Copyright © 2018 PG Forte

All Rights Reserved.

Chapultepec Press

ISBN: 978-1-880370-32-2

Editor: Maryam Salim

Cover artist: PG Forte

Dedication

This book is for Kelly, who was the first to read it back when it was just a dream.

Acknowledgments

Special thanks to Stacy Gail, Jenny Schwartz, and JK Coi, antho-sisters extraordinaire, for providing the motivation. The three of you make me want to write Christmas stories all year long!

Chapter One

I will live in the Past, the Present, and the Future.
The Spirits of all Three shall strive within me.
I will not shut out the lessons that they teach.
—*A Christmas Carol* by Charles Dickens

Detective Aldo Nash could almost hear his brain humming as it worked to categorize the myriad scents tingeing the cool night air: cedar and sea spray, dry asphalt, cooling car engine, and most potent of all, the warm, aroused flesh of the man Aldo had pinned beneath him.

Aldo slid practiced hands over the slim, partially clad form, and the man moaned softly in response, his whole body writhing instinctively closer as he arched into Aldo's touch. Aldo pulled in another heady lungful and smiled in contentment. On nights like these, he purely loved his job.

He couldn't say working undercover for the Oakland PD had exactly been a lifelong dream, but Aldo's brief stint in the army had left him uniquely qualified for it all the same, and largely unqualified for anything else. When the USA was formally dissolved following the economic collapse of the 2020s and what was left of the military was fully privatized, the idea of patriotism lost its meaning. Losing Kyle on top of that had left Aldo with no clear idea of what he wanted to do with his life.

After giving college a try, Aldo had signed up for the police academy on a whim. Unexpectedly, he found his niche. Now he derived a lot of satisfaction from knowing he was helping to prevent future crimes from happening, not just hoping to solve those that had already occurred. He got to be proactive, stay one step ahead of the bad guys rather than the other way around. But the bottom line was proficiency. He was damned good at what he did.

Not to take away from any natural ability to dissemble he might have inherited from his late actress mother, but most of his success was due, in no small part, to all the experimental drugs he'd been given by the military. His consciousness had been purposely and methodically expanded, and his brain reconfigured to the point where he could easily exert control over his brain waves and sympathetic nervous system.

In a world where just about every criminal, from the *capo dei capi* of large, multinational drug cartels to the lowliest of hood-grown thugs, had their own psi-ops tech on speed dial, that kind of advantage was a definite point in Aldo's favor. No matter how skillful said techs might be at worming their way into other people's minds and tunneling through their thoughts, with him they could only read what he wanted them to read.

Of course, there were also things about his job he didn't like. The hours were murder since, apparently, crime rarely slept and when it did, its schedule was crap. The regular debriefings with their in-no-way-optional mind-scrubs were a major headache. Literally. Worst of all, the company he was forced to keep generally sucked, and not in that good kind of way.

That wasn't the case at the moment, however. No, when it came to his present company, Aldo had absolutely no cause for complaint. Tonight's operation had him working in tandem with a new partner, an agent on temporary loan from some alphabet agency; Aldo wasn't sure which one. He hadn't asked. He didn't care. As far as he was concerned, it didn't matter. They were all pretty much the same, and the agent would be gone soon either way. Unless Aldo had missed his guess—a possibility he considered most unlikely—his new partner had been chosen for this assignment based solely on his looks. And Aldo was certainly not unhappy with those either.

He had no idea how much of the other man's appearance was due to surgical alteration or chemical enhancement, but that was something else he sure as hell didn't care about. Hot was hot, and Special Agent Caleb

Mitchell was just about the hottest thing Aldo had seen in a good long while.

Standing at a hair under six feet, Caleb was just a couple of inches shorter than Aldo. He had fair hair, full lips, broad shoulders atop a dancer's slim build, and everything about him, from his features to his proportions, was a little too perfect to be real. If the man had a flaw anywhere, Aldo had yet to find it, and not for any lack of searching. Even though they were both pushing forty, only Aldo looked his age. Special Agent Mitchell had obviously been the recent recipient of some highly classified and no doubt heavily restricted cell de-aging therapy, giving him the appearance of a man a good two decades younger than his current chronological age, the lucky bastard.

On second thought, maybe it was Aldo who'd lucked out; he got to look at the bastard, after all.

It was the case the two men were working that had brought them here tonight, to this exclusive private club located high in the Oakland Hills. Aldo's role in Operation Midas—the elaborate sting the department was running—was to attempt to infiltrate a notorious local group of wealthy, degenerate scumbags. His appearance at tonight's function, and the apparent arrest that—if everything went as planned—would shortly follow, was supposed to give him the "street cred" he needed in order to gain the scumbags' trust and acceptance. Disguised as yet another degenerate wannabe, Aldo had done his best all evening to ingratiate himself with the crew. Agent Mitchell, by virtue of his rent boy looks, had been picked to play the part of Aldo's paid escort or, as Aldo had jokingly told him, to do as he was told and look pretty doing it. He was playing his part very well, in Aldo's considered opinion, particularly at the moment.

Another gust of air blew across the parking lot. The body stretched beneath Aldo's shivered, but was it in response to the sudden chill or to the press of Aldo's fingers that had just breached his opening? Aldo leaned in closer, partially in an attempt to shield Caleb from the cool, night air, partially for the pleasure of pressing himself more firmly against that delectable flesh. "Whattsa matter, darling?" he whispered playfully in the other man's ear. "Cold?"

Caleb—bent over the hood of the shiny-new Mercedes Aldo had requisitioned for tonight's operation— glanced up at him and scowled. "Fuck you, Nash. Skip the chitchat, all right? Let's just get this over with." Up until that moment, Aldo had found Caleb's permanently raspy voice a big turn-on, but there was nothing sexy about that angry tone, the gritted teeth, the fury blazing in those jade-green eyes.

Aldo straightened immediately, his fingers slipping free of the other man's body as he pulled away from him. "What's your problem all of a sudden? Why you wanna act like such a prick?"

"Gee, I can't imagine." Caleb pushed away from the car and busied himself with his clothes, a rented tux of markedly poorer quality than the one Nash wore. He tugged his shirt and pants back into place, then bent to retrieve his jacket.

"That's it?" Aldo prodded. "That's all you got to say?"

Caleb shrugged. "Well, it couldn't possibly have been anything *you* were doing, right?" He shoved his arms into the jacket's sleeves before turning to face Aldo. "Look, don't worry your pretty little head about it, *darling*. I'm sure your technique gets you rave reviews. You're probably very popular with all the other boys."

"What the fuck is that supposed to mean?"

"What it means, Detective, is that while I have no problem helping your ass get arrested, I didn't know you'd be looking to take things so far. It's not my thing. It's not what I signed up for."

An ice-cold shower couldn't have cooled Aldo's blood any more effectively—or any more quickly either. Screwing the other man in the middle of a parking lot hadn't been his idea. Well, not entirely his idea. But it was exactly the kind of thing the character he was attempting to portray would have done, and a damn good way to ensure his arrest. Besides, they'd both agreed to it, hadn't they? Or maybe not. Caleb had been noticeably reticent during the meeting when the plan had been hatched. He'd been reticent during both their meetings. Aldo figured that was just his way. Now, as he frowned back at Caleb, niggling doubts began to displace his complacency. "Bullshit. This is exactly what we discussed. And besides, you..." A brief pause. A deep breath. A cold, hollow feeling in his gut. Fuck. He couldn't have misread those heated, heartfelt moans...could he? "You were just as much into it as I was."

"Yeah, okay, Romeo. You keep telling yourself that. Just remember, though, *none* of this was my idea."

A hot blush scalded Aldo's cheeks. "If you really hadn't wanted it, you should have said something," he insisted, striving to keep his voice cool.

Caleb quirked an eyebrow at him. "I thought I just did?"

"I meant sooner."

"What, and spoil all the fun you were having? We wouldn't have wanted that, would we?"

"Care to elaborate on that?"

"Not particularly, no." Caleb shrugged. "Anyway, I figured you already knew I wasn't interested."

"Are you fucking insane?" Aldo glared at him. "You think I knew and...and what? What the hell were you thinking? You think I'd do that kind of thing for...for *fun?*"

Caleb blinked. His expression was one of guileless innocence that had to be fake. "Well, sure. Isn't that kind of the point? Correct me if I'm wrong, Detective, but isn't that how guys like you get off?"

Nash's jaw clenched. "Exactly what are you suggesting, Agent Mitchell? What kind of guy am I?"

"Well, I *meant* gay. But you can take it any way you want. How should I know what kind of kinky shit you're into?"

"Gay? Meaning you're not?" A sardonic smile lifted

Aldo's lips. "Now, why am I finding *that* hard to believe?" He could still recall the feel of the other man's cock in his hand—stiff, throbbing, dribbling precum. There was no way Aldo had imagined that response. *Not gay, my ass.*

Caleb shrugged indifferently. "Beats the shit outta me. If I had to guess, I'd say it's probably unresolved issues from your childhood. Or maybe you just hate having to admit you're wrong." Caleb cupped his junk and stroked provocatively over the hard bulge at his groin. It was all Aldo could do to suppress a shiver of need as his gaze tracked the motion. "The way I see it, I already got one dick. It's right here, see? Conveniently placed and fully functional. So why would I have any need of yours?"

Aldo opened his mouth, ready to point out that Caleb was still hard from what Aldo had been doing to him, but before he got a single word out, Caleb's expression abruptly changed. Moving swiftly, he grabbed Aldo by the open sides of his shirtfront and yanked him close. "Incoming at two o'clock," Caleb whispered urgently. "We're about to get company, and I don't want to have to do this more than once, so let's make it look good." Then he sealed Aldo's mouth in a passionate-seeming kiss.

Aldo stiffened under Caleb's assault. What the fuck was the idiot doing now? For the space of two, maybe three heartbeats, Aldo froze, unable to even process what was happening. Then he kissed Caleb back, curving one hand possessively around the back of Caleb's neck while his other hand made itself at home at Caleb's waist. The crazy son of a bitch had him tied up in knots. His taste, his kiss, even the sounds he made, they were all so delicious, so familiar, so eerily reminiscent of Kyle. Even the scar that slanted across his midsection did so in exactly the same way as Kyle's...

Aldo had been with Kyle the night he'd received the wound that made it. He could still recall the helpless panic that had risen inside him as he pressed his hands to Kyle's abdomen, providing pressure, holding the edges of the torn flesh together as best he could while Kyle's blood welled between his fingers and his breath stuttered in and out unevenly.

"Don't die," Aldo had begged over and over while they waited for help to arrive. *"Don't you fucking do it, Kyle. You hear me? Please…"* All the while holding his gaze, not daring to look away, as though by keeping Kyle's focus he could somehow force him not to lose consciousness, not to leave him…

Aldo's thumb rubbed back and forth with an increasingly urgent motion, absently caressing the scar. Caleb shuddered again. A thick, needy whimper left his throat. His heart was pounding so hard even Aldo could feel it. When he tilted his head to the side, deepening the kiss, Caleb followed his lead automatically, tilting his own head in the opposite direction, opening his mouth wider, inviting Aldo's tongue in to plunder at will.

Yes. God, yes. Don't stop.

Footsteps echoed on the wet pavement. The soft murmur of laughter forced itself into Aldo's awareness. He tracked the sounds through the glistening fog with a growing sense of desperation. Closer… Closer… *Slow the fuck down, goddamn it!* The sooner they got here, the sooner they'd leave. The sooner this kiss would end. Aldo couldn't stand for that to happen—not yet. He didn't want this moment to ever be over. But the steady pace of the footsteps continued. Aldo heard a muffled gasp, a shuffling something that could have been a nudge, an answering grunt, then the footsteps sped up and hurried away, growing fainter and fainter until the sound had melted into the ambient distant noises. Car doors slammed. An engine started. Aldo groaned inwardly. Mission accomplished, goddamn it.

Caleb took a deep breath and pushed Aldo away. "And we're done."

Aldo's heart beat savagely. He grabbed Caleb's wrist and tugged him back against him. "The hell we are."

Caleb's hands tightened into fists. "Nash," he snarled in warning. "Let me go. I *will* deck you if you don't take your hands off me, and I mean right the fuck now."

"Not so fast. That scar on your stomach, how'd you get it?" As he spoke, Aldo pulled Caleb's shirt out of the way and held it there, exposing the other man's chest and stomach to his sight. On closer inspection, Caleb's scar wasn't exactly identical to Kyle's, but it was close enough that fifteen years and a few additional surgeries could easily account for the difference. Aldo stared at the wrecked flesh, unable to look away, remembering that long-ago fear. *I nearly lost you!* But he had lost Kyle, hadn't he? Maybe not that day, but in the end Aldo had lost him just the same.

"Screw you," Caleb growled as he yanked his arm free of Aldo's grip. "It's none of your fucking business how I got it. Now get off me."

"Tell me, please. I *need* to know."

Caleb's mouth tightened. An angry flush colored his cheeks as he dropped his gaze and looked away, mumbling, "I don't know, all right? It's not important."

"What do you mean you don't know?"

"Did I fucking stutter? I can't remember. Jeez." Shoulders hunched against the cold, Caleb tugged his shirt closed and began to button it. "Give it up already. Get a life."

"How can you not remember?" Aldo waved his hand impatiently, gesturing at Caleb's midsection. "You'd have to have been nearly gutted to end up with a mark like that." He knew that for a fact.

"Yep. Very likely." Caleb shrugged. "But what can I tell you? Another day, another mind-scrub. Know what I mean? You'd be surprised how much you can forget if you try—or, hell, even if you don't try."

"What?" Aldo's eyes widened in shock. A feeling of sick terror chilled him to the bone. "But that... Mind-scrubs? No. That can't be right." That wasn't possible, was it?

"What's the matter, Nash? No, wait, don't tell me. Let me guess. You were hoping to make a lasting impression on me, weren't you? Didja think maybe I'd be so blown away by your mad sex skills I'd change my mind and decide

I wanted to come play for your team instead? Sorry to disappoint you."

Anger flared. "You are such a fucking ass. What's your deal? Are you *always* like this? Or is this just part of some act?"

Something about Aldo's frustration must have amused Caleb. He chuckled softly as he finished tucking his clothes back into place. "You know, Nash, I think it's real cute how fixated ya are on my ass."

"Don't flatter yourself."

Once again, with no other warning, Caleb pressed close. "No need for that, is there?" he murmured, distracting Aldo with a kiss, hands fumbling at Aldo's belt. "Especially not tonight. That's what I have you for."

"Fucking asshole," Aldo groaned. The shuddering sigh that left his lips sounded a whole lot like surrender, but he just couldn't work up a reason to care. Kyle, Caleb, whoever the fuck this was, was driving him nuts. "You make me crazy. You know that, right? I can't for the life of me figure you out."

CALEB SMILED. YEAH. He knew. And right now he was counting on it. His mechanically enhanced hearing had easily picked up the crunch of car tires heading up the hill, the crackle of static from the police radios. It was showtime.

The detective's cock was still at half-mast when Caleb pulled it free of his pants. Working it back up to fully loaded and ready to pop was sinfully easy. Just a few quick strokes were all that was needed. Nash's cock pulsed and swelled in Caleb's hand as if it had been trained to it.

The fog around them had lit up like a Christmas tree by the time Caleb broke away, ending the kiss. Somewhere in the mist, car doors slammed. Nash hardly even seemed to notice that his ride had arrived. He stared fixedly at Caleb with inscrutable eyes. There was the faintest hint of a tremor in his voice as he asked, "Who are you really?"

"No one in particular," Caleb answered as he grabbed one end of the detective's white silk scarf and pulled it free. "For right now, why don't you just think of me as a ghost?"

"A-a ghost?" Nash's face went white. "Wh-what do you mean?"

"Shhh." Caleb laid a finger to his lips and faded silently back between the fog-enshrouded trees. "Not now."

"Wait. Where are you going?" Nash, his hand outstretched, took a single step forward. Then he froze as the searchlights found him.

"Hands on your head," one of the officers barked, directing his order at Nash. "And turn around slowly."

Through the heavy mist, Caleb could just make out the shocked and mortified expression on Nash's face. When his gaze dropped to his exposed crotch, Caleb knew he was debating the wisdom of ignoring the officer's order long enough to zip up his fly. The soft but unmistakable sound of guns being readied put an end to that. "Oh, fuck me," he muttered in disgust. "You son of a bitch. You set me up."

Caleb smiled. That he had. It was a cruel trick perhaps, but effective. He had no doubt it would accomplish its intended purpose of keeping both Nash and the boys in blue occupied long enough for Caleb to make his escape. By the time anyone thought to look for him, he'd be long gone, just a whisper in the wind.

Turning up his jacket collar against the cold, Caleb slipped quietly away. He'd always thought of California as being warm, balmy, even in winter. This was a helluva time to figure out that he, and perhaps most of the world, had been misinformed. He wrapped his borrowed scarf more snugly around his neck, ignoring the tendrils of heat that coiled inside him when the unmistakable scent of its owner reached his nose. He shoved his hands deep into his pockets and focused on the long walk that lay ahead of him. He was not looking forward to it.

A three-mile trek through the frosty woods wearing dress shoes, thin socks, and no coat, hat, or gloves was not his idea of a fun time. Even handcuffed, the short ride in a heated squad car, followed by a couple of hours in a cozy jail cell sounded a damn sight more comfortable. Agency protocols were crystal clear, however, and Caleb was under standing orders that left him with no other choice. The hardware in his head was considerably more valuable to the powers that be than he himself was. It was also highly classified. Under no circumstances, other than a verified medical emergency, was he to allow himself to be taken into custody or consent to having his head scanned by anyone other than agency personnel.

The fog increased as Caleb headed downhill. There was a brisk wind blowing in from the bay, and it was carrying the fog along with it. Caleb was forced to go slow and watch his step. His built-in navigational system might ensure he didn't wander too far off track or get lost in the woods, but it was of no use whatsoever against a loose rock, an exposed root, or a careless footfall. A sprained ankle would only make tonight's journey that much more unpleasant.

A car passed by unseen on the mist-enshrouded road. Probably Nash on his way to the station. A satisfied smirk curled Caleb's lips, but only for an instant, and then the memories came, bringing a wave of frustrated need. Nash's fingers inside him, twisting and thrusting until he was weak in the knees. Nash leaning over him from behind, hot skin branding Caleb's back. The taste of his mouth. The feel of his hand on Caleb's cock…

Getting fucked in the parking lot of an exclusive resort by a man he didn't even like—how could Caleb have ever thought that was a good idea? Maybe he really did need to get his head examined, just like that pretty doctor he'd been crushing on kept suggesting. Why the fuck *hadn't* he spoken up sooner? Not tonight—he was pretty sure that would have just been a good way to lose face—but way back when the operation was still in the planning stages, back when any sensible man would have demurred without having to worry about what anyone would think. Why hadn't he spoken up then?

They could have worked out something else. Lewd conduct with an apparent minor might have seemed like a sure thing, but drunk and disorderly would have done the job as well, wouldn't it? Plus, a drunken fistfight would have been a hell of a lot more entertaining and just as easy to fake as their little parking lot tryst. Or not fake, if it came right down to it. Even now Caleb's knuckles practically itched at the thought, at the opportunity to have landed a punch or two along that handsome jaw. It would not have been unwelcome. It still wouldn't be. If Nash's expression, when last Caleb saw him, was anything to go by, he probably felt the same.

Despite everything Caleb had said or implied, everything he'd wanted Nash to believe, the idea that he could be attracted to another man wasn't a total surprise. Caleb wasn't altogether certain what his original orientation had been. Maybe it had been fairly fluid from the start; it sure as hell was now. But that didn't strike him as anything strange. It just made sense, didn't it? The world was more than black-and-white, and he saw no reason to assume sexuality was any different. There had to be more to it than gay or not gay.

What did surprise him, however, was the idea he could be attracted to Nash.

Why him? From day one the arrogant asshole had done nothing but piss Caleb off. So self-righteous. So overconfident. So goddamned sure of himself. Since when had Caleb ever found that sexy? It must be nice, Caleb reflected with more than a little bitterness, to be so sure of yourself, so certain about who you were, how you felt, what you liked—*who* you liked. Caleb couldn't remember the last time he'd felt that way. Thanks to the neural interfaces in his head, his sense of self was largely rewritten with each new assignment. Maybe he'd never felt that way. Maybe he never would.

But none of that mattered tonight. None of it explained why he'd reacted to Nash the way he had, falling apart at his touch as if he'd been waiting years for the chance to do just that.

It had to be more than just looks, not that there was anything wrong with those. Nash was big, broad, buff—everything Caleb found appealing, including the neatly trimmed beard and mustache and the smoothly shaved head. But shouldn't his personality flaws have overridden all of that? Sure, he looked like someone you could count on, someone likely to be strong and dependable, but somehow Caleb couldn't believe that was the case. Look at tonight, for example. Tonight the stupid prick had even managed to turn what was supposed to have been a rather routine job into some kind of bizarre pissing contest.

No. That wasn't quite right either, was it? It was Caleb who'd done that. Unnerved by his body's reaction, he'd let instinct override common sense. He'd pulled out all the stops in an effort to find a way under the detective's skin and piss him off good. Here at the end of the night, though, the joke was on Caleb. He was the one walking home. He was the one still sporting wood.

Caleb slowed to a stop. At least he could do something about one of those factors. He paused to assess the environment. There was no one around. The road was deserted, the nearest houses were out of sight, and it was far too cold for anyone else to be out in the woods tonight. There was nothing around but trees, nothing but wood and more wood. Perfect.

Sighing in surrender, Caleb leaned back against the trunk of a large cedar. He widened his stance and quickly unzipped his dress pants. Just a few strokes—that's all it would take. Just a couple of minutes to relieve the tension, to ease the ache in his balls, to get that son of a bitch Nash out of his head and make the rest of his trek a little more bearable.

His hand felt cold as he wrapped his fingers around his dick. He brushed his thumb over the head, but there was not enough moisture to slick his way. For an instant he contemplated using spit, but it was just too cold.

Caleb pulled at his dick, quickly settling into a brisk, efficient rhythm. As he did, he cast around in his mind for a hot fantasy. Anything to take his mind off the chill. He wasn't feeling particular. Pretty much anything would do—a woman, two women, a freaking orgy. Instead the vision his mind served up was nothing like what he'd been expecting.

"Oh, fuck me," he groaned aloud as the image took hold, gathering strength, firing his imagination, becoming the very thing he needed, the only thing that was ever going to get him off tonight. He was so. Damned. Screwed.

Aldo Nash knelt on the ground between Caleb's feet. His fingers were splayed wide. His big hands clasped Caleb's hips. Bright sunlight spilled around them, and heat seemed to shimmer in the air. The landscape was beige, the air acrid and so very dry...

Caleb could practically taste the dust on his tongue. He imagined gripping Nash's head to hold him in place. The warm, stubbled texture of that almost bare skull would tickle against his palms as he fucked into that hot mouth. Alone in the woods, Caleb lifted his hand to his face and spit on his palm. He stifled a gasp as he closed his fist on his shaft once more. Closing his eyes, he imagined it was Nash's mouth— cool and wet now, as though he'd just paused to sip a cold beer. Swallowing him down. Pulling off with a twist of his lips, a flick of his tongue. Going deep again.

Caleb slid his free hand under his shirt. Palm flat, he let it coast along his abs. Let it travel slowly up to his chest. It wasn't hard to pretend it was someone else's hand stroking him like that, someone with strong fingers and a sure, confident touch. Caleb arched off the tree as he gave himself up to the sharp pleasure of fingers pinching and plucking his nipples. He thrust his hips faster, barely even aware anymore of the cold night air. So close now. Yes, God yes. He was so fucking close.

As he continued to stroke himself, Caleb let go, allowing the fantasy to spin itself out...

* * * *

He dropped his head back against the sun-warmed stone wall, felt the heat of it radiating through his T-shirt. Sweat prickled at his hairline. All at once Nash pulled off and sat back on his heels. White teeth flashed in his sun-bronzed face as he grinned up at Caleb.

"Al. Fuck, man, what're you doing? Don't stop now."

Swollen red lips stretched wider. "Tell me."

Nash's face looked different. His lips looked softer, fuller, without the door-knocker beard surrounding them. His face looked softer too. Rounder. Gentler. Younger maybe? Caleb shook his head. "Fuck you, man."

"Yeah, you'd like that, wouldn't you?" Nash leaned in and ran his tongue up the underside of Caleb's shaft, then pulled back again. Caleb reached for him, but Nash knocked his hands away and sat back again. "Nope. Not happening. That's all you get until you tell me what I want to hear."

Caleb's heart pounded. The muscles of his thighs and butt tensed and released, tensed again. So close. So, so close. "Fucking cock-tease."

"Yeah, but you love me for it."

Caleb groaned again. He punched the stone wall behind him until his fists felt bruised. His cock was achingly stiff, but he wouldn't touch himself. Rules of the game. There was no way he'd give Nash that satisfaction.

Without taking his eyes from Caleb's face, Nash groped on the ground till he found the beer he'd been drinking earlier. He brought the bottle back to his mouth again, but he didn't take a drink. Not right away. First he teased the opening, licking, circling, spearing the hole with his tongue. When his lips finally closed around the thick rim, Caleb's eyes nearly crossed.

Nash turned his head slightly to one side, still holding Caleb's gaze. He lifted his chin, giving Caleb a clear view of his throat as he drank deeply, swallowing gulp after gulp. Caleb's knees went weak as he watched Nash's throat work, watched his Adam's apple bob, imagined what it would feel like, those muscles massaging his cock...

"Fuck. You win, okay? I need it. Now."

Nash lowered the bottle. His eyes gleamed warmly as he wiped his mouth with the back of his hand. A triumphant smile curved his lips. "I don't think I heard that correctly. Need what?"

"I need your mouth on my dick; what do you think?"

Still smiling, although not as widely now, Nash shook his head. "And you think that's the way to get it? Sorry, but no."

"C'mon, man, what more do you want?"

"You know. But hey, take your time. I'm in no hurry. I'm fine where I am. I can stay here all day if I have to."

Privately Caleb doubted that was the case. The ground was too hot, too rocky, too hard on the knees. Nash had to be feeling it by now. But he was a stubborn shit. Caleb couldn't help but admire him for that. He groaned again and chuckled weakly. "Bastard. It's you. All right? I need you. Only you."

"You got that right, darling. And don't you forget it. Now, come to papa."

Nash leaned in, ready to take Caleb in his mouth again, but suddenly that was no longer what Caleb wanted. Reaching down, he hauled the other man to his feet, then spun around to pin Nash to the wall.

Nash melted against him, going suddenly boneless in Caleb's embrace. His arms snaked around Caleb and held him close, damp skin to damp skin. It should have been uncomfortable, but Caleb reveled in it. Their lips met in a hungry kiss at about the same time Caleb succeeded in finally freeing Nash's erection. Just like tonight, it sprung to attention in Caleb's hand with hardly any coaxing. He fisted both their cocks together and began to stroke with a fast, urgent rhythm. "Now who's the papa?" he muttered against Nash's lips.

"You are," Nash gasped as he tore his mouth away from Caleb's. "Always. That's why I..." He broke off, struggling for breath. "Oh God, Kay, stop a minute."

Nash's arms went lax. He pulled back just far enough for their gazes to lock. The look in his eyes was too turbulent, too intent, too rife with meaning. Caleb's hand faltered and fell still.

Nash swallowed hard. "Look, I don't care how many girls you wanna get with, okay? Fuck 'em all, if you have to. Get it out of your system. Just—"

"Shut the fuck up," Caleb ordered. He pushed forward and slanted his mouth over Nash's again. "Just stop talking." He closed his eyes and kissed Nash. Hard. Bruisingly hard. Anything to shut him up. Anything to make him stop looking at Caleb that way. "Besides, it isn't... It's never been... That's not it, okay?" It had never been about getting it out of his system. That was never going to happen. It didn't matter how much either of them might want it; Caleb couldn't change who he was any more than Aldo could. "Why don't you get that?"

"Whatever," Nash growled as his arms tightened around Caleb once again. "Just remember one thing, asshole: you're mine."

You're mine. Two words that tripped Caleb's switch, lit his fuse, and sent him hurtling over the edge. "Right back atcha, babe," he murmured incoherently as he resumed his task, stroking them both into oblivion. In no time at all, his muscles seized and his balls drew up and white light flashed behind his eyes. He came hard. So hard he took Nash with him. They groaned as one, their faces buried in each other's necks, their spurting cocks bathing them both with sticky seed...

* * * *

Warm liquid splashing over Caleb's ice-cold fingers pulled him back to reality. He opened his eyes, still struggling to pull air into his lungs. In the wake of the strangest damn fantasy he'd ever had, he felt dizzy and drained and...what the fuck was that about anyway? He shivered with a sudden chill as the wind knifed through the thin fabric of his shirt. His skin was sweaty and damp. The smell of his spunk was strong in the cold night air. And the sense of urgency was almost overwhelming. He had to escape, had to get away right the fuck now, back to town, back to civilization, back to something approaching normal. STAT.

He cleaned his hands off as best he could, but they were still a little sticky and they still trembled faintly as he pulled his clothes together. He turned up his collar, shoved his shaking hands into his pockets, and headed downhill. If tonight had been a contest, it wasn't hard to decide which of them had won.

Chapter Two

Three-quarters of an hour later, Caleb was glancing around the ER. It was quiet tonight, somewhat surprising for this time of year, he supposed, but good for his purposes. It should make it all the more easy to spot his prey, Sally Evans, the doctor who'd treated him when one of his aural interfaces shorted out last month. She had to be here someplace, and he had to find her before time ran out. Her shift was almost over. She was about to get off work for the night, about to start a two-week vacation; if he didn't catch her before she left... Well, he didn't even want to think about that.

He cast another look around. This would have been easier if she were a man and tall enough to stand out in a crowd, but she wasn't. She was petite and curvy with silky platinum hair cut pixie short in the back but longer on top and in the front. He'd thought about her hair a lot these past few weeks. He'd thought about how it must look first thing in the morning, or after she'd been walking in the wind, or poking up through his fist as he tugged her head back and pushed into her from behind...

It was probably a mistake, thinking things like that. Given the way he looked right now, it would be a miracle if she was interested in him. The only reason he stood any chance at all was because she'd treated him, she'd viewed his charts and his X-rays and read the heavily redacted reports describing his condition. She knew he wasn't a kid. Whether that would be enough, however, only time would tell.

"Caleb?"

Her voice behind him had him turning to face her. "Hey. Sally. Just the woman I was hoping to see." Though he'd steeled himself for the impact, the sight of her still took his breath away—the mirror-smooth gleam of her hair, the bright aquamarine of her eyes, the swift, surprised smile that stretched those luscious lips. "How's my favorite doctor doing tonight?"

"What are you doing here?" Her smile dissolved, and a small frown furrowed her brow as she looked him over. "What's wrong? You're not having another reaction, are you?"

Caleb shook his head. "No, it's nothing like that."

"Oh. Well, good. That's...that's good." She nodded absently. Caleb thought she seemed distracted, as though her thoughts were elsewhere. Definitely not a good sign. What did he really know about her anyway? Maybe she had a boyfriend, a husband, a family to go home to. Maybe what he'd taken for friendly interest had merely been professional courtesy.

Sally cleared her throat. "So are you here about some other problem then?" She'd seen him several times since that first night. He'd been in for tests, a follow-up visit, and half a dozen unscheduled stops just to say hi. Just because something about her smile warmed him. Just because something in the glances she'd occasionally sent him had seemed to suggest an interest that wasn't purely professional. Or purely platonic. But all those other occasions had been during regular hours. She was probably wondering what he was doing here now, in the middle of the night. As well she might.

Caleb shook his head a second time. "No. No problems," he said again. "I'm fine, really. It's just...well it's been kind of a rough night, if you know what I mean."

Sally's eyes narrowed abruptly. "What do you mean 'a rough night'?" she asked as her gaze raked him from top to bottom. "You look like you've just come from a party."

A party. Right. Caleb's jaw clenched. "Yeah. Something like that."

Sally's frown deepened. "Okay, well...look, I hate to cut this short, but I'm afraid my shift's just about over now so..."

"I know. That's why I'm here."

"Oh. It...it is?"

Caleb groaned inwardly. Admittedly it had been

awhile since he'd attempted something like this, but was it too much to hope that he wouldn't completely suck at it? "I was hoping to catch you. I wanted to try and convince you to come out and have a drink with me."

A pretty pink blush colored Sally's face. "Th-that... I mean, thank you. I'd like that very much, but I'm afraid it's impossible. Caleb, you know I can't go out with you. You're my patient."

Caleb shrugged. "No offense, Dr. Evans, but I think you're overstating the case. I have plenty of doctors, more than I want, and I see them all the time. What you and I had was an emergency, not a professional relationship. It's not like we're seeing each other on a regular basis. Yet."

"All the same—"

"Not that I'd mind, you know," he said, hurrying on. "I mean, the only reason I kept coming back here after the first couple of times was to see you. So what I guess I'm saying is, I'd really like to see you regularly, just not professionally."

Sally shook her head. "I can't." Caleb took courage from the fact that she looked genuinely regretful.

"Okay, how 'bout this. What if I promise not to ever get sick again while you're on shift—will that work?"

"Caleb..."

"C'mon, Sally. What would it hurt? We're talking about one drink, not a lifetime commitment. Besides, it's the holidays. Can't you make an exception for that?"

Sally's mouth twisted into a grimace. "The holidays. Right. Don't remind me."

Caleb's eyebrows rose. "Uh-oh. Sensitive subject?"

She shook her head. "No. Just a long story."

"Really? Well, I have time. I'd love to hear it."

"I'm sorry, Caleb. I can't go out for a drink with you. For one thing, it's late. For another...where would we go? Given the way you look, I can't believe anyone would even serve you a drink in the first place. I'd probably end up being charged with corrupting a minor or something."

Caleb's eyes widened. He hadn't really thought about that. "You're right. I can't believe that hadn't occurred to me. But at least you can see now that I don't do this very often. So...I know. How about a cup of coffee? Dessert? Pie or something?" Hell, everyone liked pie, didn't they?

"It's not that I'm not flattered," Sally replied. "But c'mon, Caleb, what are you thinking? Why me?"

Caleb smiled at that. "Well, now that's a strange question. Just look at you." His gaze grew heated as he took his own advice. His date in the woods with his hand and an imaginary lover might as well have been days ago rather than hours. He really, really wanted to change her mind. "I can't believe you don't have half the men you work with running after you. Not to mention a few of the women. You're beautiful, talented, intelligent, kind. Plus you know 'the real me.' Not many people can say that."

"I seriously doubt that's true. Besides"—she waved her hand to indicate his appearance—"look at *you*. You're the one people should be running after. You should be hooking up with girls who are... What I mean is... Oh hell."

"Girls who...what? Who look more my age? Like, teenagers, d'you mean? You know better than that. How well do you think that would work out for me?"

Sally shook her head. "I guess it wouldn't."

"Damn right it wouldn't. Hell, even if I had a mind to, I couldn't date girls who look the age I do."

"Fine. I misspoke. That still leaves a wide range of women who are older than teenagers and still younger than me."

"So? What am I supposed to talk about with these women? What do I even have in common with them? As it happens, I find experience and maturity very attractive in a woman."

That brought a reluctant smile to her lips. "Oh, thanks...I think."

"Ouch." Caleb laughed. "Okay, I think I'm not helping my case any, am I? I should probably just shut up now, but just for the record, that was meant as a compliment. Maybe I miss what I used to have. Maybe sometimes I don't want to have to think about how I look on the outside. Because you know what? It doesn't match what's in here." He pointed at his chest.

Sally nodded. "I know. You're right and… Maybe we all feel that way."

"Maybe we do. But forget that for now." He took a deep breath. Might as well lay it all on the line. "Here's the thing. I like you, Sally. I've been thinking about this for a while, but tonight… Well, like I said, it's been kind of a crappy night, and I just wanted to relax after everything that's gone on and…and not think too much. Not have to pretend I'm something or someone I'm not. And you were the first person I thought of." He shook his head. "No. Scratch that. You know what? Even if you don't want to go for a drink with me right now, that's cool because I'm already feeling better just having talked to you for a few minutes here. But…" He shrugged. "Call me greedy, but I want more. I want a chance to get to know you better."

Sally sighed. "Again, I'm flattered. And I'd like to get to know you better too. Maybe some other time, okay? Let me think about it. Right now…things are complicated. It's the holidays, like you said, and that's just not a good time for me."

Caleb nodded. "Yeah, okay, I can respect that, but listen, if you're only saying that because of my looks—I mean if that's what you're worried about, if your objection has to do with how we'd look together or if that's what's making this 'not a good time' for you—then I kind of wish you'd let me know right now so I won't waste any more of your time. Or mine. Because there's a good chance I'm going to be stuck looking like this for quite a while. So if the way I look is a problem for you…"

"I get it." Sally glanced away.

She looked so…sad. Caleb was sorry he'd pushed her, sorry he'd probably ruined the easy friendship they could have had otherwise. He'd had to try, and he'd meant every word he said, but he was really going to miss her.

"I don't know. I…" She stopped again and shook her head and finally met his gaze. "Would you like to come back to my house for that drink?"

Caleb's eyebrows rose. "Sure. Do you mean it?"

She nodded and smiled, but her smile seemed uncertain and a hint of sadness still lingered in her eyes. "Why not?"

"Then yes." Caleb smiled. "I'd like that very much. Thanks."

Sally nodded. "Okay, well…good. Let me just finish up here. Do you want me to text you my address and you can meet me there?"

A flush heated Caleb's cheeks. He suddenly felt every bit as young as he knew he looked. Maybe even younger. "Actually, would you mind giving me a ride? As it happens, I sort of walked here."

"You walked?" She looked him over again. "Like that? You're not exactly dressed for the weather. Weren't you cold?"

Caleb sighed. "You have no idea."

"All right, well, why don't you have a seat?" She waved a hand toward the waiting room chairs. "I'll be back as soon as I can, and then we'll see what we can do about warming you up." She flushed a little as she said it. As if she hadn't wanted to be so blunt.

Caleb did the gentlemanly thing and pretended not to notice. "Thank you," he answered gravely. "That would be much appreciated."

* * * *

Sally began second-guessing her decision to bring Caleb home with her the minute she stepped foot in her apartment. Even as she stood in the entryway and toed off her shoes, she could feel the tension building between them—and not in any kind of way she'd call good. He stood silent beside her, glancing around, taking everything in. Was it only her imagination, or could she really feel him growing colder and more distant with every second that passed? Maybe it was nothing. Or maybe it was her.

It had seemed so simple back at the hospital. Why not keep each other company tonight? Why not forget the past, forget tomorrow, forget her embarrassment at being seen with someone who looked so much younger. And most of all, why not forget, for just a little while, the fact that Christmas was coming—her first Christmas as a widow. Why not just get together with someone fun and gorgeous, someone who seemed to like her for all the right reasons, and fuck each other into cheerful oblivion? It was just one night. What would it hurt?

But now, much as she still really wanted to do that, much as she'd love to carry on with that agenda, she wasn't sure she could. How could she make love with him—or anyone for that matter—here in the home she'd shared with her husband? Or in the bed she still wasn't able to sleep in, now that she was on her own? Most nights since Davis's death, she ended up on the couch or huddled on the chaise lounge in her bedroom. She slept fine in either of those places. In fact, she slept fine anywhere else—even at the hospital, surrounded by noise and activity and endless rounds of questions. Yes, Davis was gone. Yes, this would be her first Christmas without him. And no, she had no idea how she was going to cope with his absence. The same way she'd coped all these months, she supposed, which was to say: not well at all.

Even with all of that, however, she could still sleep there. But here? In their home? In their bed all alone? No. Just no. She couldn't do it.

And since she hadn't reclaimed the bed for herself, she could hardly take anyone else in it either. It would feel like cheating, which sounded stupid, even in her head, but there it was. Irrational or not, that was the way she felt, and it was a huge mood killer.

Maybe they could fuck on the couch. That would be simple enough, wouldn't it? After all, they both liked it rough. Wasn't that what he'd said? So maybe Caleb could just bend her over one of the arms and take her from behind. But no, on second thought, that wasn't what he'd said either, was it? A rough night…that could apply to so many things.

He'd made no actual mention of blindfolds or restraints. There'd been no talk of whips or safe words or discipline. That had merely been her overheated imagination at work. Not that it mattered anyway, because she didn't think she could do any of that with him either.

So what if it was the kind of thing she and Davis might have done? What she'd had with Davis was different. That was them. Maybe someday she could go there again, either with Caleb or with someone else, but not tonight.

Tonight, despite all the hot and dirty fantasies she'd been having about Caleb these past few weeks, she couldn't follow through on any of them. She couldn't ask him to take her up against the wall or on the dining room table, the kitchen counter, the shower, the floor. All the places she'd been thinking about. Not for their first time. If it was going to happen tonight, it would have to be in bed. Which meant…it wasn't happening.

The realization made her sigh, and even her breath came out sounding shaky, uncertain. Crap.

"Are you nervous about something?" Caleb asked.

Sally forced a smile in an attempt to turn it into a joke. "Why? Should I be?"

"I don't know. That's why I'm asking."

Right. She shook her head. "No. Of course not. Everything's fine." She gestured toward the couch. "Look, why don't you have a seat, okay? Make yourself comfortable. I'll go get us something to drink. Is wine all right?"

His gaze met hers. He stared searchingly at her for a moment longer, then shrugged. "Sure. That sounds perfect. Thanks."

Caleb had removed his jacket by the time Sally returned with their wine. He looked so sexy slouched comfortably in the corner of the couch. The sleeves of his white shirt had been rolled to just below his elbows, and she couldn't help but admire his forearms, golden hairs catching the light as he reached for the glass she offered him. She could already imagine what those arms would feel like wrapped around her, what those hands would feel like caressing her skin. She shivered a little at the thought.

"Cold?" Caleb asked as she sank onto the couch beside him.

She shook her head and sipped her wine, already at a loss for words. No wonder he'd claimed not to know what to say to the twentysomethings she'd suggested he date. Even knowing how old he actually was wasn't helping her any, was it?

Caleb glanced around again. "So. No decorations. That kind of surprises me."

"Does it? Why?" She followed his gaze around the room as she thought about Christmases past. Usually she loved everything about this time of year, especially the decorating—the tree, the lights, the stockings. Davis had always loved it too, always made it fun. Taking everything down again? Yeah, not so much fun. This year, however, Sally had been unable to work up even the smallest amount of enthusiasm for any of it. Who needed a tree when there was no one to leave presents underneath it for?

"I don't know." Caleb shrugged. "I guess because you seemed like the type."

"Oh, there's a type?" Sally settled back on the couch and regarded him with amusement. "Please. Enlighten me."

"I just... Well, look around you. It looks like you've been able to make a home here." Caleb's expression was somber as he gestured at the room around them. "That's not something everyone can do. It's something I haven't had in...well, as long as I can remember, actually." For a moment a wry smile curved his lips, then was gone again. "I guess I figured the two kind of went together. But maybe I don't know what I'm talking about?"

"No, I think you might be right about that. I just haven't been in a very festive mood this year."

"Really? Why's that?"

Sally smiled. "I'm afraid *that* is part of the long story I'm still not ready to talk about," she said as she reached over and removed the glass of wine from his hand. He looked at her questioningly. "As a matter of fact, I think we've talked enough altogether."

She lifted a hand to frame his face. His eyebrows rose, his gaze faintly questioning. Smiling at his hesitant expression, she leaned in and touched her lips to his. Just a soft kiss, almost chaste, but she felt the thrill of it clear to her toes. She pulled back with a breathless gasp, but his hand was on her waist by then, his eyes hot on hers as he urged her to him with gentle pressure. Closer. Closer. Until she was practically straddling his legs.

His mouth sought hers again, his tongue teasing her lips until she opened for him. He wrapped an arm around her waist, while his other hand slid up her back, pressing her closer. Sally looped her arms around his neck and relaxed into his embrace. Long, long minutes passed while they explored each other's mouths. Her breasts felt heavy, ripe, aching for his touch. She wanted more, wanted his teeth on her skin, his fingers on her clit, on her slick and swollen folds, wanted his cock deep inside her. Her pussy pulsed with need, and she rocked her hips. His hand slid higher, fingers caressing the back of her neck, cupping her head, tangling in her hair. Her scalp tingled in anticipation, but his touch stayed tender. *More.* Groaning softly, she pulled her mouth away from his, offering her throat instead. His lips grazed her neck, the slight stubble of his beard lightly scraping against her skin. And still she needed more.

"Wait," she murmured, pushing suddenly at his chest.

He let her go and eyed her solemnly. Until she reached for the hem of her shirt; then his face relaxed and he smiled in appreciation as she pulled the shirt over her head and tossed it away.

Caleb's gaze heated as he looked her over. When she tried to melt back against him, he held her away. "Not yet," he said, his voice husky and deep. His fingers skimmed her flesh, lightly tracing the swell of her breasts above the lacy edges of her bra. "Let me look at you."

He hooked a finger in the silky material and lowered one cup. Sally's pulse thundered in her ears as he leaned forward to tease her nipple with his tongue. She arched her back and pushed herself closer in blatant invitation. *More.* A whimper tore from her throat when he finally took the tight bud in his mouth. She closed her eyes to better feel the sensations, squirming with her need for release. She felt him slide her bra strap down her arm to free her other breast. When he covered it with his palm, she pressed herself even harder against him. *Yes. More!*

Somewhere close at hand, her phone began to ring. The noise barely registered in her mind.

"Don't answer it," Caleb muttered against her breast, and for a moment she had no idea what he was talking about.

"No," she agreed at last. "Hell no. Whoever it is, they can... Oh fuck." Her mood plummeted, and she twisted away, scrambling to extricate herself from his arms. "Let me go, Caleb. I have to get that."

"What?" He glanced sharply at her even as his hands dropped away. "Why's that? Is it work?"

"No," she answered as she grabbed for it. "I just...I just do; that's all." There was only one person who'd be calling her this late. He was the only one who knew how depressed she'd been feeling lately, and if he couldn't reach her, he'd probably assume the worst. He'd be over in a flash, if that were the case, breaking the door down if he had to, just to make sure she was okay. "Hey, babe," she said, gulping in air, sounding only a little bit breathless. "What's up? I didn't think I was going to hear from you tonight. You just getting off work?"

Caleb pushed away from the couch—probably giving her a modicum of privacy. She shot a grateful glance in his direction, touched by his consideration. It was hard enough trying to keep her voice level, to sound calm and collected. She'd never be able to pull it off if he was still touching her. But oh, she wished he was touching her just the same. Her body burned with need, and she had to squeeze her thighs together to get even a little relief. She tugged her bra back into place, hoping it would help her focus on the voice coming through the phone. She was mostly succeeding until Caleb bent to press a kiss against her head.

She glanced up at him again, startled to see that he had donned his jacket and shoes. "Hold on a sec," she said into the phone and quickly pressed mute. "Caleb? You're not... What are you doing? You're not leaving, are you?"

"I think I'd better." He shrugged and gestured at the phone. "It's getting late and you're obviously busy, so..."

"Busy? No. I'm not... Wait. That's not..."

"Maybe another time. Call me, all right?"

"Caleb, stop. Please. Let me explain."

He shook his head. As his gaze roved over her one more time, she could read the regret in his eyes, but his expression was firm. His mind was obviously made up. "No need. I think I get the picture. Don't get up. I'll just let myself out."

She stared after him, too surprised to move, too exasperated to speak. What would she say, anyway? Disappointment crashed over her. The sound of her front door closing had never seemed so grim. It took almost a minute before she remembered she was still on the phone.

"I'm back," she said, trying and failing to sound cheerful, cringing a little at how pathetic she sounded instead. She pulled the blanket off the back of the couch and wrapped it around her. It couldn't take away the chill, of course, because that was mostly inside her.

"Everything all right over there?" She could hear the caution in his voice. The hint of suspicion.

"S-sure." She shook her head in helpless confusion. It had been all right, hadn't it? Up until a moment ago. Or so she'd thought. She sighed again, propping her head on her hand, trying hard not to cry. "No, actually. Not really."

"Want me to come over?" Even through the phone she could hear his worry, his concern. She almost smiled. "You can make me some coffee and tell me all about it."

"Yeah, okay," she said, nodding even though he couldn't see it over the phone, blinking away her tears of self-pity, trying to compose herself. "Sure. You do that."

Chapter Three

Aldo made it to Sally's apartment in record time. He didn't even bother knocking. He simply let himself in using his own key. As he pushed the door open, he was relieved to smell coffee. He glanced down the short hallway and was even more relieved when he caught sight of Sally seated on her couch, looking more composed than she'd sounded when he talked to her on the phone and with no more tears in evidence.

"Hey, babe," he said, raising his hand in greeting. "It's just me." Not waiting for an answer, he detoured into the kitchen to pour himself some coffee before joining Sally in the living room. The apartment looked cluttered. Unusually so. Which was something he probably should have noticed months earlier. He would have too, if he hadn't been grieving himself. He frowned. It didn't look like she'd moved a thing since Davis's death, merely left everything as it was and piled more stuff on top of what was already there.

"What the hell, Sal?" He threw her a pointed look. "This place looks like a freaking mausoleum. What're you doing? Trying to bury yourself along with him? Can't you at least get someone to come in and dust for you once in a while?"

He'd been hoping for a wince, hoping to shock her into feeling something. Her only response was a disinterested shrug, which didn't improve his mood in the slightest. Even her hair seemed dull, totally lacking its usual otherworldly gleam.

Fuck, he was tired. He collapsed on the couch and pulled her against him, wrapped an arm around her for good measure. "Thanks for the coffee, by the way," he said as he took a bracing sip.

"You're welcome."

Aldo sighed. "Okay, so what's up? Something happened tonight. What?"

"Nothing really." Sally craned her neck to glance up

at him. There was a hint of challenge in her gaze. "It's just...I brought a guy home with me. Is that what you want to know? You keep telling me I need to start dating again, so fine. I did."

Aldo didn't say anything at first. He had to fight to keep his emotions from showing on his face—he didn't want to scare her, after all—but goddamn it. Yes, he wanted her to date. He'd hoped that might make her feel better. He sure as hell hadn't wanted it to make her feel worse. If it turned out someone had taken advantage of her vulnerability, if someone had hurt her, he'd track the bastard down and gladly rip him a new one. "Why do I get the feeling you're only willing to credit me with the idea, all of a sudden, because it was a mistake?" he asked at last, trying his hardest to make it a joke even though they both knew it wasn't.

"I don't know why you'd think that. I didn't say it was a mistake, did I?"

"Didn't have to." Aldo studied her for a moment longer, then asked, "Who was he?"

"That's not important. It's no one you know, so..." She shrugged. "He said he wanted to get to know me better. We came here. It should have been easy, but then..."

Aldo felt his blood begin to boil. "Then...what? What happened? C'mon, Sal, do I have to drag every damn word out of you?"

"Would you quit acting all big brothery? Just be supportive and shut up. I don't know what happened, all right? Everything seemed fine. We were getting to know each other, and then...well, then you called."

"Me?" Aldo winced, remembering her initial hesitancy on the phone. "Fuck, Sally, don't tell me you sent him away because of something I said? I didn't *have* to drag my ass over here tonight. If you were busy, you should have said so."

Sally's lips thinned. "Don't you think I know that? And I didn't send him away. I didn't need to. He did that all on his own."

"Did what?" Aldo swallowed another mouthful of coffee. This was making no sense, and he was starting to get irritated. "Why don't you just tell me what happened?"

"I'm trying to, aren't I?" Sally nestled a little closer, winding an arm around his waist. Her hair teased his neck when she shrugged. "And anyway, I dunno what happened. Everything was fine. I mean, I think it was. I felt ready, you know? I've known him for a little while now and tonight... It seemed like a good time for this. We were both on the same page: both attracted to each other, both interested in taking things a step further, but then...when we got back here and I...I couldn't..."

"Are you fucking kidding me?" Aldo's arm tightened instinctively around her. He was startled by the blast of anger, by the raspy growl that emerged from his throat. "Are you saying some son of a bitch got ticked off and walked out on you because you wouldn't sleep with him? Who is he? Tell me where to find him, and I'll fucking kill him."

"Aldo." Sally turned her head to glint up at him. "Would you stop it? You would not."

The words were matter-of-fact, but Aldo wasn't certain if that was confidence he heard in her voice or a hint of challenge. Either way, it pissed him off. He arched one brow. "Oh no?"

"No. I know you. And I wouldn't want you to anyway. That's not what happened, okay? It just...it didn't work out; that's all. No harm, no foul."

"You don't even know what that means, do you?" He hated that plaintive tone in her voice. She sounded like a lost little girl when she used it. And she clearly didn't know him anywhere near as well as she thought she did. He wasn't always the nice guy she imagined him to be. Davis hadn't been either, for that matter. He doubted anyone was. She was still too naive, too innocent. And he'd be damned if he was going to be the one to change that. She was the only good thing in his life. And their friendship was still the only relationship he had yet to fuck up. It was damn sure gonna stay that way if he had anything to say about it. Still it made him mad. "What the fuck is wrong with this guy?" he groused. "He couldn't cut you some slack, give you a little time? Doesn't he realize how much you've been through lately?"

Sally sighed. "Of course he doesn't. How would he know?"

"You didn't tell him? How come? I thought you said you'd known him for a while?"

"A few weeks—yeah. And of course I didn't tell him. How would that go? What was I gonna say? 'I know you think you want me, but what you don't understand is that I'm a pathetic little widow who can't figure out what she wants.'"

"Stop that. You're not pathetic."

"Oh, babe." She shook her head. "I am, you know. I'm not blind. My life is running away without me, and I can't seem to stop it and…half the time I don't even care. I'm tired of fighting it, tired of feeling lost. If that's not pathetic…"

"It hasn't been that long," Aldo pointed out a little desperately. "You have to give yourself time. Maybe *you're* the one who needs to cut yourself some slack?"

Sally chuckled weakly. "So says the man who, just last week, told me—yet again—that it was time for me to move on."

"Yeah, well…" He broke off, sighing. "Sometimes I don't always think things through before I speak. You know that."

"Or before you act."

"Yeah. That too." Davis had made the point frequently, had given Aldo hell on a regular basis for his hotheaded, impulsive ways. He'd always claimed Aldo would get himself killed one day if he didn't change. And yet it was Davis who was gone too soon.

"I miss him."

Aldo nodded, eyes closing for a moment as a wave of pain crashed over him. "I know, honey. I do too."

Sally sat up again and looked at him, studying his face. He met her gaze a little warily, not sure what he'd find there. Anger? Recrimination? He and Davis had been partners, damn it. It had been his job to keep him safe. But Sally just looked sad, sad and lost, and that was even worse.

She framed his face with her soft hand and kissed his cheek. "Yeah. I guess you do. We're quite a pair, aren't we?"

"That we are." Aldo sighed as Sally curled up against him again, this time laying her head in his lap. There was no point in lying about his feelings now. He'd never made a secret of how he'd felt about Davis. Not to Sally, anyway. She'd known about that for years. Even before Aldo had introduced Davis to her, she'd known. Maybe Aldo should have resented that. Maybe it should have bothered him how easily his best friend had fallen for the man he'd wanted. But what would have been the point? He was pretty sure she hadn't set out to do it. It had just happened. They'd always had similar tastes in more than a few areas. Their tastes in men were no exception.

Besides, although Davis might have been the perfect man for Aldo in all other ways, he had one, insurmountable flaw: he could never return Aldo's feelings. Davis wasn't attracted to men. And Aldo was never settling for second place with anyone. Not ever again. Not after Kyle.

So if it wasn't Sally who snagged Davis, it would have been some other woman who ended up with him, who won his heart and took him away from Aldo. And maybe that would have been better, because then he wouldn't have had to see it every day—he wouldn't have had to see *them* every day. But maybe it would have been worse. At least this way, he and Sally still had each other. Neither of them was alone, and they got to share their grief.

"It doesn't matter why he left," Sally said musingly.

For a moment Aldo had no idea who she was talking about. He frowned in confusion. "What?"

"Tonight. Maybe I wasn't as ready as I thought I was. Maybe he could sense that."

"Yeah, maybe." Or maybe not. Aldo was still pretty sure the only thing this guy, whoever he was, had sensed was that he wasn't getting laid. Bastard. He lifted his cup to his lips, but the coffee was gone. When had that happened? And why hadn't he chosen a bigger mug? "At least you tried, right?" he told her as he wedged his empty cup between the cushions and the back of the couch. He stroked her hair. "At least you're getting out there. You're making an attempt. I'm proud of you, Sal. Davis would be too. You know he'd want you to get on with your life."

"Yeah." Sally let out a gusty sigh as she reached down and scooped a white scarf up off the floor. "You're right. And I know I'd feel the same way about him if the roles had been reversed. I'd want him to go on and be happy. But I feel so stuck, and I just…can't. I can't."

"You can't *yet*. C'mon, Sal, have some faith. It'll get better. You know it will."

"I know," she answered, but she didn't sound it. Not even a little.

"Have you made any plans yet for the holidays?" he asked as he watched her play with the scarf, running it through her fingers again and again.

She shook her head. "No."

"And you're still taking time off, right?" She always did this time of year. He'd thought maybe this year she'd choose to bury herself in her work instead. He'd been hoping she'd find some way to keep busy.

"Yep. Tonight was my last night."

"Well, then, we should do something. C'mon, why not? Let's head up to the cabin for a few days. It would be good for you. It would be a good break for us both, to get out of the city, for at least a little while."

"I thought you had to work?" She shifted onto her back, her head digging into his leg a little as she moved. "Aren't you supposed to be in the middle of something?"

Aldo shrugged. "Yeah, well…I could still get away. You know, if you wanted to."

"I don't know. It sounds tempting, but I think I just want to be alone."

That was flat-out not going to happen. "Oh yeah? Since when? You didn't want to be alone tonight, did you?"

"No. I didn't. And look where *that* got me." Sally groaned and closed her eyes. Lifting her arms, she draped the scarf across her face like a blindfold, like she was attempting to shut him out.

Aldo scowled. It looked like a fucking shroud. His fingers itched to snatch it away. He debated the wisdom of leveling with her, of giving her fair warning. There was zero chance of her spending the holidays alone. Either she was going up to the mountains with him, or he was camping out here on her couch. He'd lost one good friend already this year. He was not losing two.

Sally blew out a heavy breath. Air fanned the edge of the scarf, drawing Aldo's attention. A shock of recognition twisted his guts. *It can't be. No fucking way.* He sat up fast, dislodging Sally from his lap in the process. He plucked the scarf away from her. "Where the hell did you get this?"

"What?" She scrambled to her knees, staring at him, her face a mask of confusion. "What's wrong? Why are you so upset?"

"This scarf." He studied it closer. His. It was his. Had to be. What the fuck? "Where did it come from?"

Sally turned her attention to the scarf. "I don't know. Maybe Caleb left it? He was in kind of a hurry to leave." Her lips twisted a little on the last part, as though it hurt to think too much about it. "I might have mentioned that fact a time or two."

Aldo's temper spiked. He tightened his hand on the scarf, crushing the silk. Oh, if only it were still around that asshole's neck. "Caleb...Mitchell? Are you telling me *that's* who you brought home with you?" It wasn't possible. It wasn't even remotely possible. But what other explanation could there be?

"Yeah, why?" Sally's eyes widened in surprise.

"Wait. You know him?"

"Know him?" Aldo bit back a laugh. "Yeah. You could say that."

Sally blushed crimson. "I know what you're thinking. He's not as young as he looks."

"So I've been told." Aldo shook his head. That two-timing son of a bitch. "I guess he's really not gay after all."

"Caleb gay?" Sally frowned. "Why would you think that?"

"It's nothing. Never mind."

"Wait. He's not, is he? Is that why he wouldn't sleep with me?"

"I just told you he's not, didn't I? It's just...I kind of got the feeling—earlier—that he might be, but then he went home with you. So no, he clearly isn't gay. And I don't know what the hell I'm talking about. Ignore me."

Sally gnawed the edge of her thumbnail. "I'm not so sure. You usually do know things like that, don't you? When you get those kinds of 'feelings' about people, aren't you usually right?"

Aldo laughed. "'Cause why? Gaydar? I thought you didn't believe in that?"

"I don't. It's got nothing to do with that. I'm talking about being very observant. Which you are."

"Well, thanks, but like I said, obviously this time I was wrong." Nothing new about that, was there? Aldo retrieved his coffee cup and picked up Sally's empty as well, and took them both back into the kitchen for a refill. For good measure he added a hefty dose of brandy to both cups. There had to be something wrong with him, he decided as he returned the living room. Otherwise, why did he always fall for guys who were never going to return his feelings?

"How'd you two meet anyway?" he asked Sally as he crossed back to the couch, mostly to change the subject.

"Thank you," she said, accepting the cup from his hand. "We met at work. He came into the ER to get checked out." She took a sip, and her eyes widened in surprise.

"Really? What are you, playing doctor now? Do I look like I need medication?"

Aldo smiled. "I think we both need it." He sat back down on the couch, and then the rest of her response kicked in. "Whoa. Time out. Wait a minute."

"What now?"

"Since when do you date your patients?"

Sally's cheeks went red once again. "He's not my patient. He's just... I just met him there, okay?"

"So how'd you know he wasn't a kid?"

"I saw his charts."

Aldo studied her thoughtfully. There was no reason for her to be studying the charts of random patients. Clearly there was stuff she wasn't telling him. "What happened to him? How did he end up in the ER?"

"Aldo, you know I can't tell you that. It's confidential. Doctor-patient privilege and all that."

"Yeah? I thought you said he wasn't a patient?"

Sally's lips pursed. She took another sip of coffee. "Well...not now he isn't."

"Whatever. Just tell me one thing. He said he can't remember stuff—things from his past. Injuries. People. Is that true?"

Sally nodded. "I would imagine so. It certainly seems reasonable."

"How? We're talking about major stuff. And don't give me any more of this 'confidential' crap. It's important, all right? I really need to know."

"Well, I don't know how much I can tell you." She held up a hand to still the protest that was on his lips. "Not because I don't want to, because I don't know very much myself. I know he sustained extensive injuries in the past, substantial enough to require reconstructive surgery. I know the various...modifications he's been equipped with have radically altered his brain waves. I'm sure 'difficulties with his memory' is the least of the challenges he's had to face."

Aldo gulped a mouthful of coffee, ignoring the burn.

It was nothing next to the sudden chill that had gripped him. "What kind of reconstructive surgery? You mean on his face?"

Sally nodded. "As well as other places, yes. Now it's your turn. How do you know him?"

Good question. "Actually I met him the same way you did."

"At the hospital?"

"No, silly. Work. The department has had him on loan these past few weeks."

Sally's eyes narrowed as she looked him over. "Were you with him tonight? He said it was a bad night. Did something go wrong? Are *you* okay?"

Aldo smiled faintly. He was warmed by her concern, but the last thing he ever wanted to do was make her worry. "Yeah, hon. Of course I am. You know me, right? When am I ever not fine? And I don't know what he had to complain about either." Thinking about it left him vaguely resentful. "Stupid bastard," he muttered under his breath. If anyone had a right to be pissed off about how tonight's operation went down, it was Aldo.

"Do you two not get along? Do you think that's why he left?"

"How's that? Did you tell him it was me on the phone or something?"

"No, but maybe he heard you and recognized your voice and then left so as not to run into you again. He has implants in both ears, you know, so his hearing is off the charts."

Good to know. Aldo nodded gravely. *But not really a surprise. And doctor-patient privilege my ass.* "Well, you would know that kind of stuff better than me."

Sally placed her cup on the coffee table, then lay back down with her head in his lap. "You're not going to get all weird about this, are you?"

He rubbed at the frown lines between her eyes. "Weird about what?"

"Me and Caleb. If I decide to see him again?"

"Were you planning on seeing him again?"

"I don't know." She dropped her gaze and murmured quietly. "Maybe. I really like him, you know."

Perfect. Just what his already craptastic night had needed. Aldo forced a smile. "No worries, hon. We're solid. Same as always, right?"

Sally nodded, then covered her mouth to hide a yawn. "Okay, good."

"You're tired." Aldo stroked his fingers through her hair, brushed the stray strands away from her face. "Want me to leave so you can get some rest?"

"No." Sally yawned again. "Unless you want to. Why don't you stay for a while? Maybe watch some TV or something. I'm just going to take a little nap."

"Okay. I'll stay." Aldo kicked off his shoes and propped his feet on the coffee table. It wasn't the most comfortable setup he could think of, but he'd slept in worse conditions. If it made her happy, it was worth it. He picked up the TV remote and flipped slowly through the channels. Hanging out like this, late at night, just the two of them, reminded him of the earliest days of their friendship.

He'd first met Sally when he returned to college shortly after he'd used up a big chunk of his inheritance resigning early from the military. It might not have been the smartest use of his money, but his heart and soul had been raw. He'd seen too much, done too much, lost too much: his parents in the food riots, Kyle in…some pointless battle or other. He couldn't continue. He'd needed to get out, no matter how much it cost.

Once upon a time he knew soldiers received training as a matter of course. In the new pay-for-hire army, however, rank, pay, and privileges were dependent on training and training was paid off over time. Or, if you were wealthy enough to afford it, with cold, hard cash.

Once he was out, Aldo had found himself at loose ends. He'd had no idea what he wanted to do with the rest of his life. School seemed a good place to try and find out.

Sally was younger by a few years, and he'd been attracted to her right from the start, just not romantically. She was tiny and energetic and still so fucking sweet, even despite having lost almost as much as he had. Something about her wide-eyed optimism, her genuine compassion, brought solace to his jaded soul and brought out the protective side of his nature.

Maybe he'd needed someone to take care of at that point. Maybe he'd needed to prove he could care for someone and not let them down. Maybe Sally was like the baby sister he'd never had, or maybe caring for her was as close as he dared come to being in love.

He'd never made a secret of how he felt. Sally had known they were never going to be more than friends, but she'd fallen in love with him all the same. They'd never spoken about it—neither of them had dared—but he knew. It had taken them awhile to sort through that tangle of emotions, and he'd been worried he would lose her too. Med school had helped with that. She'd been too focused on her studies for a real relationship and too exhausted, whenever they did get together, to do more than hang out anyway. And then came Davis.

Aldo was already in love with Davis, his very straight partner, when he introduced him to Sally. It was hard watching the two people he cared most about fall for each other, but it would have been hard watching Davis fall for anyone, and he never begrudged them their happiness. If anything, it helped assuage a little of his own guilt over not being able to return Sally's feelings.

Since Davis's death, however, that guilt had returned full force, compounded by his failure to save Davis, leaving him with a heightened feeling of responsibility for Sally. And an increased need to keep her in his life. He knew Davis would want him to keep her safe, and that's just what he intended to do. Maybe he couldn't save his partner, but he'd damn sure save his partner's wife.

Chapter Four

Caleb stood on the deck of the isolated cabin, taking in the snowy mountain scenery. Tall trees surrounded the chalet-style cedar cabin. Their tops brushed against the sky, empty now except for a lone hawk, circling high overhead. In the distance, far below, between the trunks of the snow-dusted pines, Caleb could just make out a sliver of water shining in the sunlight—a shimmery greenish blue, the same color as Sally's eyes. So this was Lake Tahoe. A nagging sense of familiarity teased the back of his mind as he breathed in the frosty air, but it was nothing he could place. About the only thing that was clear this morning, aside from the sky, was the realization that his preconceived vision of what constituted California weather had just been skewed even further out of whack. This place was about as far from the warm, surf-side paradise he'd been imagining as it was possible to get. Just like this house was as far from the kind of cabin he'd been expecting anyone at Nash's pay grade would be able to afford—even if it was nearly a century old. Apparently the "cabin" had belonged to the detective's family for several generations.

And if this had been the house where the family had gone to "get away from it all," Caleb wondered what kind of mansion they'd lived in the rest of the time. Not that it was any of his business, of course.

Caleb hunched his shoulders against the cold, burrowed deeper into his borrowed jacket, and promptly cursed its owner once again. Goddamn Nash. His scent lingered in the coat's shearling lining, torturing Caleb with memories from three nights ago. He lifted his arm to sniff at the sleeve, drawing in another deep lungful, until the sudden tightness in his jeans drew his attention to the absolute stupidity of what he was doing. If Caleb wanted to hold on to any shreds of his sanity—or his already diminished self-respect—he'd simply have to stop wearing the other man's clothes.

Unfortunately that might not be an option. At least not until the stores reopened after Christmas and he could buy some new clothes. He hadn't packed for this sort of weather, and since freezing his ass off until then was definitely *not* part of his plans either, he supposed he'd have to find some way to deal with it—preferably a way that didn't involve him having to excuse himself to go jerk off every few hours.

He still didn't know why Nash had wanted him here, but he'd bet anything the other man was working some kind of angle. He'd been sure of *that* ever since the morning, two days ago, when the subject had first come up.

* * * *

"Mitchell, I have a bone to pick with you."

Caleb glanced up in surprise from the report he'd been typing. Heat flared at the sound of Nash's gravel-voiced growl. What was it about the guy that always sent Caleb's heart racing? And what was his problem now? It was the morning after Caleb had left Nash to face the music in the parking lot and yeah, he'd expected the detective might be a little annoyed by the impromptu change in plans, but Nash was a big boy. Surely he could handle a little embarrassment, couldn't he? If the murderous fury in his face was anything to go by, maybe not.

"Oh, gimme a break, Nash, would you?" Caleb snapped, glaring right back at him. "Get over yourself already. Why you wanna overreact like this? It was no big thing, all right?"

"N-no big...*thing*?" The shock and outrage in the detective's voice caught Caleb off guard. *What did I say now?* It took him a moment to make the connection. When it did, he couldn't keep his face from betraying his amusement. *Oh, for fuck's sake.* Caleb smirked as his glance strayed involuntarily to the front of the other man's slacks. It figured the guy would assume he'd meant it *that* way!

"Sorry. Didn't mean to offend. I'm sure it's perfectly adequate. I mean, unless your boyfriends are all size queens or something, in which case, maybe not."

Nash's wrathful expression switched to blank confusion for an instant before changing back to mad-with-a-side-of-mortification. "Asshole. I'm talking about Sally."

"Huh? How d'you know about—"*Fuck.* "Oh, hey, whoa!" Caleb eyes widened in dismay. He held up his hands. "I thought she was single. Swear to God, man. I would never have asked her out if I'd known you had an interest there."

Nash rolled his eyes. "I'm not dating her, dipshit. I'm gay, remember? We're just friends. And she is single—now. She was married to my partner."

"Your...partner? Really? How's that working out for the three of you?"

"Not domestic partner. My partner here at work." Aldo rapped with his finger on the desk Caleb had been assigned to. "The dude whose desk you're sitting at. Show some respect."

Caleb regarded him solemnly. "What happened to him?"

Nash glanced away, his expression suddenly weary. "Same kind of thing that generally happens. He got in front of a bullet. Been gone for almost a year now."

"I'm sorry."

"Yeah." Nash nodded. "Sure. Everyone's sorry. Doesn't change anything, but thanks just the same."

"So what's the problem with me seeing Sally then? Is it just me you don't like, or don't you think she should date anyone? Or do you think it's just too soon?"

"I don't have a problem with her dating. And that's for her to decide. She's a grown woman. If you're what she wants, that's her lookout. My problem is the way you walked out on her last night, right in the middle of...of whatever the fuck you two were in the middle of."

Caleb grinned at that. "Eloquent."

"Shut the fuck up." Aldo pinned him with another

glare. "I care about her, all right? And in case you haven't figured it out by now, she's vulnerable. She just got back into the dating game, and it hasn't been easy for her. Last night... Well, let me put it to you this way: you hurt her again like that, and I will come after you. And then...big thing, little thing, it ain't gonna matter much what size you happen to be packing, 'cause I'm gonna rip it right the fuck off you altogether."

Before Caleb could even formulate a response to that, they'd been joined by Nash's captain bearing Grinch-worthy gifts from the city of Oakland. Apparently Nash's hearing had been delayed due to the holidays, which was not what any of them had wanted. That meant the rest of the operation was on hiatus until after the New Year as well. Even better, despite Caleb's hopes that his services would no longer be needed, he'd been informed that the department expected him to stick around—until otherwise notified, and mostly twiddling his thumbs, by all accounts—on the off chance it might become necessary for him to reprise last night's role sometime in the future.

"Excuse me, Captain, but what am I supposed to do with myself until then?" Caleb protested after she'd cautioned him he was expected to stay in character for the duration—thereby dashing his newfound hopes of pursuing a relationship with Sally.

"I would imagine you'll probably want to stay out of sight as much as possible, Agent Mitchell," Captain Douglass replied, her sweet tones at distinct odds with the steel in her gaze. "But if you'd prefer to take your gay-for-pay butt downtown and park it on one of our streets somewhere in hopes of picking up some spare change, that's entirely your own business. Just don't get arrested for it. Detective Nash's character can afford to post bail. I'm afraid yours can't."

Ouch, Caleb thought as the captain walked away. It looked like Nash wasn't the only one who'd taken offense at Caleb's improvisational rewrite of last night's op. Either that or the old girl had the hots for Nash and didn't like it that

Caleb had hung her pet out to dry. Not that it mattered, of course. He was screwed either way.

Nash stared thoughtfully at him for a minute, then asked, "So you got any plans for the holidays?"

Caleb snorted. "I guess not now. Thanks so much for pointing that out."

"Yeah, so, since you won't be busy, why don't you come up to Tahoe with me and Sal?"

"Excuse me?"

"I have a cabin up in the mountains, just outside of town." Nash smiled. "Nice place. You'll even have your own room. I don't know if you ski or not, but even if you don't, there's still lots to do. It's quiet, peaceful, and—added bonus here—it'll keep your ass off the streets."

Caleb's eyebrows rose. "Why, honey, asking me to go away with you? So soon? What kind of boy do you think I am?"

"I don't know yet." The look Nash fixed on him was far more serious than Caleb had expected. "That's still up in the air, which is kind of the point. If you're gonna be dating my best friend, I damn sure intend to find out. This'll just make that easier. Besides, you know, there's a lot of wilderness up there. If it turns out I don't like what I learn about you, I'm sure I can find the perfect place to hide your body."

"Funny," Caleb muttered. "So seriously, I still don't get it. Five minutes ago you were threatening to castrate me if I made another wrong move where Sally's concerned. Now you're inviting me to go away with the two of you. What's up with that?"

"It's like I said, it'll give us all a chance to get to know one another. Besides, I figure Sally will like it. And you do owe her for last night. I thought maybe you'd want a chance to make it up to her. That makes sense, doesn't it?"

Not even a little, Caleb thought, which should have been reason enough for saying no. But Nash had him dead to rights about wanting to make it up to Sally for his behavior the night before. He should have stuck around. He should have at least given her the chance to explain instead of jumping to conclusions. Everything in her apartment had screamed couple, however, and that had put her reluctance to be seen with him in public into a very different light. He'd been stupid, and if he turned Nash down, he'd be spending the next couple of weeks alone with his regrets. There was no upside to that.

"But hey, maybe you've got a better idea. If so, forget I mentioned it."

Caleb glanced away, shrugging a little as he said, "No, it's cool. Getting out of the city for a while sounds like a plan. I could go for that. Thanks."

"Don't mention it."

"So I guess I just have one more question for you then."

"Yeah?"

"I'm wondering, given the situation and all, whose pimp are you acting as here—hers or mine?"

Caleb had to give him credit. Nash didn't even blink at that remark. "Why, yours, of course, Mitchell," he said, clapping a hand on Caleb's shoulder. "After all, you are the rent boy in our little scenario."

* * * *

"It's pretty up here, isn't it?"

Caleb turned as Sally came to join him at the railing. She was wearing a fuzzy sweater—mostly purple, but with bright bits of pink and gold and olive green mixed in that made her eyes look even bluer—over snug jeans and carrying a steaming mug of coffee. In the sunlight her hair looked almost iridescent. "Yeah, it is," he said, smiling at her. "And it's just gotten prettier."

That got him a smile in return—one of those knowing, secretive smiles all women seemed to do so well, full of mystery and promise—and a softly spoken, "Thank you."

"Thank *you* for letting me barge in on your vacation like this. I hope I'm not intruding?"

Amusement sparkled in Sally's eyes, and another pretty blush climbed her cheeks. She took a sip of her coffee and then said, "Aldo didn't tell you, did he?"

Uh-oh. "Tell me what?"

"I only agreed to come because he said you'd be here."

"What?"

Sally shrugged. "He'd been pestering me about it for weeks, but I guess I thought it would be too depressing. You know, just the two of us, sitting around feeling sorry for ourselves? I know he thinks he needs to take care of me, but he didn't have to spend his holiday doing that." She glanced at him and smiled. "But then he told me you were coming up here with him and…"

She trailed off, eyes gleaming, cheeks even pinker than before. Caleb felt his chest tighten in alarm. "I'm not *with* him," he hurried to explain.

Sally ducked her head. "I know that. Or…at least I hoped that was the case. After you left the other night, I have to admit I wasn't completely sure."

Caleb sighed. "I know. I'm sorry. I shouldn't have run out on you the way I did."

"Yeah." She put her coffee down, leaned her forearms on the railing, and turned her head to look at him curiously. "About that. What happened there? I thought things were going pretty well and then…?"

"They were." He placed his hand on hers. "You know they were. It's just that I didn't know about your husband at the time. And then when I saw your home…I guess I got it in my head that you had a boyfriend who was maybe out of town or, I dunno, maybe you two had had a fight or something, and I didn't want to get in the middle of that. I mean, I couldn't get in the middle of that. You know who I am, but it's not supposed to be common knowledge. But then you kissed me, and I stopped caring about that. Until the phone rang and…" He broke off with a shrug. "I should have given you a chance to explain."

Sally nodded sadly. "I know. You should have. And I should have told you about Davis. Aldo said the same thing."

Aldo again. Caleb straightened away from her. "Sounds like you two are really close." He couldn't believe how much that fact bothered him.

Sally nodded. "We are. He's my best friend."

"And you met him through your husband?"

"Other way around. I've known Aldo since college. He's the one who introduced me to Davis."

"I see." *Aldo. Davis.* Caleb suppressed a sigh. He loved the way her tongue caressed their names. He'd give anything to hear her say his name like that. "I guess I'm confused. I thought he was older than you."

"He is. But only by a few years. He was in the military for a while. He went back to school after opting out."

"Oh yeah? Where? What branch?"

"I don't know." Sally picked up her mug again and took another sip. "He might have mentioned it once. Probably he did, but I don't remember and he never talks about it. Something happened to him there. I don't know what other than that it left him disillusioned about pretty much everything—but *don't* tell him I said that. Like I said, he hates talking about it."

Her words barely registered. Caleb's attention had gotten caught up in the way her tongue traced over her lips. The need to kiss her again had been building inside him ever since he'd left her apartment the other night. Now it all but overwhelmed him. He shifted closer. Her eyes widened in surprise when he took the mug from her hand and set it on the railing, then grew dark as heat and understanding took the place of surprise. Her lips curved upward, and that was all the invitation he needed.

He gently caged her face in his hands. As he bent his head, her mouth opened on a soft sigh. She tasted of coffee and cinnamon and woman, a lush, spicy flavor that went straight to both his heads. He groaned as he wrapped an arm around her back and pressed her close. He couldn't get enough of her. From the way her hands clutched at him, crushing fistfuls of his jacket, he had the feeling maybe she felt the same. As she went up on her toes, her hips brushed along the length of his erection, stroking him through his jeans. Even that slight contact was enough. He sucked in a quick breath as desire knifed through him.

He cupped her butt in his hands, and then he lifted her against him, intent on grinding his hips into hers. A soft whimper left her lips as she slipped her arms around his neck and teased his tongue with hers. He had never been sorrier for all the layers of clothes that separated them. Despite the fact that they were outside in broad daylight and it was cold as hell, he'd have had them both undressed in an instant—if he could only figure out how to do it without breaking her hold on him or breaking their kiss, or without taking his hands off her for even a second.

It took the sound of a door slamming open and a loud voice announcing, "Hey, c'mon. Breakfast!" to shake Caleb back to his senses.

He lifted his head. His gaze immediately locked with Nash's across the width of the deck. Nash stood just outside the cabin door. His hands were fisted at his sides, and an odd, angry-looking flush was on his face. There was a look in his eyes Caleb couldn't decipher, even with his enhanced vision. What was that? Anguish? Longing? Jealousy? Need? It was gone before he could figure it out, if it had even been there at all.

Certainly Nash's voice sounded nothing but jovial as he demanded, "Are you two at it already?" He spread his hands wide and arched one brow and looked pointedly at Sally until she giggled and hid her face in the front of Caleb's jacket—for which reaction Caleb totally owed him. "I can't leave you alone for a minute, can I?"

"Oh, sure you can," Caleb replied, loosely folding his

arms around Sally. "In fact, why don't you just go back inside? Go back to doing whatever you were doing and let us get back to doing…whatever we were doing," he added, consciously echoing Nash's own words to him at the station the other day. He wasn't ready to give this up yet. He was enjoying it all too much—the way Sally felt nestled against him, the way she fit so perfectly in his arms. This was why he could never give up women entirely—or part of the reason, anyway. It didn't matter if a handsome man could turn his head from across a room or across a redwood deck. It didn't matter that, right now, for example, the sight of Nash, with his thin navy pullover and well-worn jeans stretched taut over his muscular frame, made Caleb's mouth dry, made his knees feel unacceptably shaky. Made him feel altogether too conflicted. Nash needed to leave. Now.

"Hey, if you want to stay out here all day, it's your call," Nash answered, those broad shoulders rising and falling in a small shrug that only served to focus Caleb's attention even more firmly on them. "No business of mine. Just so you know, though, breakfast is ready, and I have a lot of other cooking to do between today and tomorrow, so if you don't come in now, you'll be eating it cold."

"All right, you win." Sally turned her head to smile at Nash over her shoulder. "We'll be there in a minute."

Caleb tightened his grip, loving the way her head felt pressed against his chest, loving the way her hair tickled his chin. "Better make that two minutes."

Sally looked up at him and grinned. "Or better yet, three."

Aldo rolled his eyes, shook his head, and went back inside, leaving Caleb to wonder when, in the last two minutes, "Nash" had become "Aldo" and why it was that the sight of him walking away should leave Caleb suddenly feeling…bereft? Why was he suddenly wanting to call him back, wanting to draw him into a three-way kiss?

"So," Sally purred as soon as the cabin door closed and they were alone once more. "Where were we?"

Caleb glanced down at her and smiled, refocusing his attention. "Somewhere right around here, I think," he said as he cupped his hand around the back of her neck. He loved the way she slipped her arms around his neck once again, loved the feel of her body against his as she rose up on her toes.

He sighed in contentment as he settled back into her kiss. He could be wrong, but he was pretty sure they were going to miss breakfast.

Chapter Five

Aldo slammed the skillet he'd been using into the sink and started scrubbing viciously at the cast iron, not caring in the slightest that he was absolutely ruining the cookware's painstakingly seasoned surface. When exactly had he lost his mind? How in the world could he have ever imagined inviting Caleb here was a good idea? And how the fuck was he going to get through the next two weeks without embarrassing himself?

Here was yet another example of how his stupid tendency to act before completely thinking things through had come back around to bite him in the butt. At the time it had all made sense. Now he couldn't help but wonder what his original motives had actually been.

In part he knew he'd been desperate to keep Sally safe. It didn't sit well with him that she was planning on isolating herself over the holidays. That wasn't at all like her. That sounded just a little too much like scary-depressed, slit-your-wrists-in-the-bathtub behavior. He wanted her somewhere he could keep an eye on her and make sure nothing like that happened, and he wasn't particularly picky about his methods.

If having Caleb here would do the job, surely that was reason enough to invite him, wasn't it? If Caleb could do for Sally what Aldo couldn't, if he could bring her some joy, help her get over her grief, help her move on with her life, that was even better. That was well worth putting up with the annoying prick for a couple of weeks.

But did "annoying prick" really encompass all Aldo thought about the man? He had to admit it didn't. Beyond the fact that he was hopelessly attracted to the other man—on a purely physical level—there was also this nagging suspicion in the back of his mind. Although perhaps suspicion wasn't the right word to use. Call it a hope. A hunch. Or plain old wishful thinking.

What if Kyle hadn't been killed as reported? What if

some part of him had survived and been rebuilt? What if there was a chance of bringing him back?

Just the thought that there could maybe be some sort of second chance, that he and Kyle could finally find closure, had brought the memories bubbling to the surface of his mind. That was another reason he'd wanted Caleb here, to see his reaction to the cabin and the surrounding area. Would he remember any of it from the time Aldo and Kyle had spent here a decade and a half earlier?

There hadn't been any indication that he had, even though Aldo had given Caleb the bedroom they'd shared all those years ago. Everything was pointing toward the conclusion that Caleb was no more than what he appeared, and that Aldo had set himself up for two weeks of needless suffering.

This morning especially, Aldo really had to wonder if he wasn't inconveniencing himself to no purpose, putting himself out of his room, sleeping in the cabin's open loft, acting like a guest in his own home. No, not a guest, more like a fucking servant. Or, just like Caleb had suggested the other day at the station, like some kind of pimp.

His mood, already lousy to begin with, had gone seriously south when he'd caught sight of the two of them kissing on his deck. He hadn't thought about how that would affect him. Now he knew. It was like getting kicked in the chest after you'd already been knocked to the ground, or reopening old, old wounds that had never really healed. It had been like walking in on Kyle all over again, finding him lip-locked with some woman at a party, or on the beach, or even—in what had been the final straw—in what was supposed to have been *their* bedroom. It didn't even matter that, this time around, Aldo had no reason to feel cheated on, or that it was Sally who was being kissed, or that she'd looked happier than he'd seen her in months—which was all he'd told himself he wanted. If anything, that only made it worse.

What if Caleb and Sally became a couple after this?

What if Aldo's brilliant lack of a plan resulted in his having to spend not days or weeks, but months or years or even decades watching the two of them kiss. It had taken him long enough to get over the anguish of seeing Sally and Davis together like that. And he'd never even kissed Davis. They'd never even touched, other than in the most platonic ways. Whereas Caleb…

Maybe he was overreacting. It had only been a few days, after all. Maybe the memory of Caleb's mouth on his, of Caleb's body stretched beneath him was a transitory thing, something that wouldn't stay with him, something that would simply fade away. He wouldn't want to bet on it, however. Not the way his luck tended to run.

Footsteps on the deck were the only warning he had that his solitary sulk was about to be invaded. It gave him just enough time to compose himself, to call up all his training, just as he'd had to do earlier on the deck, and hide the way he was feeling. There was no way he could allow either of them to catch a glimpse of that. He couldn't risk the inevitable questions. He was pretty sure neither of them would approve of his hidden agenda. Hell, at this point in time, he didn't approve of it himself.

"You mentioned something about breakfast?" Caleb asked as he followed Sally into the kitchen. Aldo couldn't help but suspect Caleb was enjoying this all a little too much. As though he could somehow tell how upset Aldo was. As though he knew how much Aldo wanted him, and was taking pleasure in thwarting him. It was exactly the kind of thing Kyle would have done. The heartless prick.

Aldo leveled his best "I've got my eye on you" glare at the other man, then nodded toward the table, crowded with what should have been a mouthwatering display of pancakes and bacon and a bowl piled high with fresh clementines. Loneliness struck him suddenly. *Oh, fuck me.* What the hell was he doing now? He wasn't just acting as a pimp anymore either, was he? Apparently he'd also assigned himself the roles of butler, maid, and personal chef. Maybe he should just think of all of this as an elaborate Christmas gift for Sally? The Lord knew, she needed something to make her feel better. Maybe Aldo would just have to suck it up and take one for the team.

"Thanks, babe," Sally murmured as she slipped by him to pour herself more coffee. "It looks and smells wonderful."

Aldo nodded in acknowledgment. "You're welcome. Now go eat before it gets cold."

"Aren't you going to eat with us?" she asked just as Caleb wandered over to join them.

"Sure." Aldo turned back to the sink and muttered, "Soon as I finish cleaning up."

"I'm pretty sure that skillet is about as clean as it's going to get," Caleb pointed out, leaning over Aldo's shoulder, leaning in too fucking close. "I didn't think you were even supposed to put those in water—just wipe them down. Isn't that the case? Seems to me I heard that somewhere along the line."

Aldo's heart skipped a beat. The warmth of Caleb's body, especially noticeable since he'd just shed the jacket he'd been wearing, played havoc with Aldo's senses. He had to consciously slow his heartbeat down, had to struggle against the instinct to lean back against Caleb's chest, had to struggle against the need to sink into fantasy. Caleb's arms around him. Caleb's warm hands slipping under Aldo's shirt, sliding up to caress his chest, toying with Aldo's nipples. Or, even better, those same hands moving lower, slipping into the waistband of Aldo's pants...

"Why don't you both just go away now? Sit down and get started, okay? I told you, I'll be there when I'm done."

"C'mon," Sally urged, laughter obvious in her voice as she tugged Caleb away. "Better do as he says. I guess Aldo's in his grumpy bear mood again."

"Really?" There was a hint of playful laughter in Caleb's voice as well as he followed Sally across the room.

"Aldo's a bear? I had no idea."

The "bear" closed his eyes and prayed for strength and the quick return of his sanity, which must be missing altogether now—along with a good portion of his hearing. Because suddenly he was "Aldo" not "Nash." Suddenly it sounded a lot like *not-gay* Caleb, who was supposed to be here for *Sally*'s benefit, was flirting with *him*. That couldn't be right, could it? On the other hand, why the fuck should he be surprised? When had being with Aldo ever kept not-straight Kyle from flirting with anything in a skirt?

And if maybe-Kyle ended up playing Sally the way actual-Kyle had played Aldo? Aldo would *absolutely* knock the bastard into the middle of next week.

"Al! C'mon already. Sit down and eat. Why don't you let me deal with cleaning up? It's the least I can do."

Yeah, it sure as hell was that. "Fine," Aldo snapped. "I'll be right there." Still, he took a moment to carefully dry the pan he'd been mishandling and replace it on the stovetop. He was going to have to reseason it right after breakfast, although preferably not while Caleb was at the sink.

Then the rest of Caleb's speech reached Aldo's brain. Al. He was Al now? Oh hell no.

Not that it meant anything—not really—but *no one* called him that. He was Aldo frequently, Nash even more often, but Al? Not once in fifteen years had anyone called him that.

He took his seat at the table, trying hard not to assign a deeper meaning to the nickname or the more troublesome question of why. Why now, after weeks of calling him Nash, had Caleb suddenly broken with his own protocol? Was it anything more than a normal response to being here in Aldo's house, eating his food, sleeping in his bed? Or was there a deeper meaning to it all?

As they settled down to their meal, Aldo could not keep his gaze from straying across the table, watching Caleb, watching his hands as they peeled the skin from a clementine, as they popped the sections into his mouth, searching for some hint of recognition. He could not get over it. All the little details, all those things you never really notice about another person, but still you think you'll never forget...

How was it he'd never taken the time to pay attention?

One thing he could not help noticing, however, were all the curious glances Caleb kept casting around. There was a faint frown on his face, and Aldo found his heart beating faster once again. Maybe Caleb did remember something. Maybe Aldo wasn't just imagining things. Finally he couldn't keep from asking, "So, Caleb, you haven't said. What do you think of the place?"

"Oh, it's great," Caleb answered, suddenly seeming very involved with his pancakes. "Very comfortable. I guess I'm just a little confused."

"By...?"

"Well, it's Christmas Eve, right? And from the way you both talk about it, I'd've thought you'd make a pretty big deal of the holiday, and yet..." He glanced around again. "Why no decorations?"

"I think Aldo is just trying to be considerate of my feelings," Sally suggested, her cheeks coloring as she said it.

Aldo shot her a quick glance. "You only *think* so?"

"I told him a few weeks ago I didn't feel like doing anything special this year, that I just wanted to hide until it was over, but now"—she met Aldo's gaze and smiled wryly—"maybe that was a mistake."

Aldo blinked in surprise. Well, hell. He refocused on his breakfast to hide his relief. "There're some decorations in the attic. If you two want to knock yourselves out putting them up, it's fine with me." On second thought he wasn't sure how fine he really was. He hadn't exactly been feeling all that Christmasy himself.

Of the three of them, Davis had always been the most enthusiastic about the holidays. So when Sally had expressed no interest in acknowledging the season this year, Aldo had thought nothing of it. At least at first. It wasn't until later, after he'd put that together with her plans to isolate herself, that he'd become worried. If she'd been planning on simply working through the holidays—like he'd wanted to do—he wouldn't have thought twice about the matter.

"What about a tree?" Caleb asked. "Any chance you got one of those in your attic?"

A tree too? Aw, hell. Aldo suppressed a wince. He looked at Sally. "You *sure* you're okay with this?"

She thought for a moment, then nodded. "Yeah, I think I am. I think it would be good."

Yeah, freaking awesome—not. Aldo nodded. "There's a tree farm not far from here," he told Caleb. "Sally knows where it is. I'm going to have my hands full today between cooking tonight's dinner and getting a head start on tomorrow's, but if it's what you two want to do, go ahead and take the truck, make a day of it."

* * * *

Aldo puttered around the kitchen for a short while after the others left, but the ghosts of Christmas past were haunting him today, making him wish he'd never mentioned the damned decorations in the attic. The last time he'd used them had been several years ago when Davis had decided he was in the mood for a white Christmas. They'd come here then, and just like now, Aldo had handled the cooking while the others had dealt with the decorations. He should have thought about that when he'd suggested coming up here again this year, but they'd spent Christmas here so infrequently, he'd honestly thought it would be better. Right now, however, he was second-guessing a lot of his decisions. Maybe the fact that he and Sally had made fewer memories here gave those few an added luster, making them seem even more precious.

Finally giving in to the inevitable, he went up to the loft. If anyone was going to mess around up there with the boxes he and Davis had so painstakingly packed away, if anyone was going to fuck with his memories of that particular afternoon, it was going to be him, damn it, and no one else.

The crawl space was just what its name implied; one had to be on one's knees to access it. The whole time he was pulling boxes out, Aldo was remembering the afternoon he and Davis had put them in there. Most particularly he was remembering—vividly—how he'd spent most of that time ogling Davis's ass and indulging in a harmless little fantasy of what it would be like if he and Davis were the married couple and Sally was simply their really close best friend. The three of them were already so at-home with each other, very little would have to change. If he and Davis were married, they would still be up here together packing boxes away while Sally was busy downstairs, vacuuming up pine needles. The only differences would be who got to go home together, which of them ended up sleeping alone, who would have to keep his hands to himself. It would all be exactly the same, except…

Alone in the loft, seated on the floor, surrounded by boxes, Aldo gave in to the grief that had come out of nowhere to broadside him again. God, he missed Davis so much—his smile, his laugh, the sound of his voice, all the little things he could never get back. The torture Aldo had lived with for years, of always being around Davis yet knowing he'd never really be *with* him, was nothing compared to this. He'd trade the two in a heartbeat if he could, and never regret it.

If only he and Sally could have been more than friends. How many times had he thought that over the years? If they'd fallen in love with each other instead of with Davis, it would have saved them both so much heartache. There'd never been any question in his mind that he loved her. He enjoyed the time he spent with her, would be devastated if he lost her, and had no doubt whatsoever that he'd want her in his life forever, but that didn't make them lovers. From an aesthetic standpoint, he found her arrestingly beautiful. He loved looking at her, loved watching the play of light on her skin, but that didn't mean he craved her either. He didn't hunger for a taste of her. When they danced together, he felt no urge to grind against her; his hands didn't itch to roam places they shouldn't. If there'd ever been any doubt in his mind as to whether he was gay or whether Kyle had been a liar, that alone would have convinced him of the facts. Because if Aldo wasn't attracted to Sally, whom he loved, how could Kyle have loved Aldo as much as he'd claimed and yet still have been so irresistibly drawn to women?

And now there was Caleb, who Aldo would *not* make the mistake of falling for, no matter how attractive he found him. He'd learned that lesson, damn it, not once, but twice already. Judging by what Aldo had observed this morning, Caleb was absolutely attracted to women—to Sally in particular—which meant Aldo had been deluding himself these past weeks thinking Caleb was attracted to him. Which meant he'd be putting his feelings for the man on lockdown if he knew what was good for him, starting right this fucking minute.

Chapter Six

The tree farm hadn't changed much since the last time Sally had been there, not that there was any reason it should. Life went on. That was a lesson she probably should have learned sooner. Although in her defense, maybe it wasn't the kind of lesson you could ever get in one go-round, but rather the kind of lesson you just had to keep relearning. Each loss came wrapped around its own fresh pain, bundled up with the same lessons all over again, and maybe only stopped when you breathed your last.

Still, as they wandered through the rows of trees, she found a surprising level of comfort and even a grudging sense of peace in the fact that so little had changed. The gravel still sounded loud beneath her boots. The crisp winter air was still heavily scented with pine. The man beside her still held her hand in a sure, warm grip. And no, it wasn't Davis. It would never be Davis again. But she had to come to terms with that, didn't she? Or she'd be crippled forever by grief.

Maybe if she didn't dwell on the facts too much, if she could stay in the moment and try to remember that the ability to take pleasure in today took nothing away from those other days, those other years, that other man who had once walked by her side and held her hand, then maybe she could find the perfection that was *this* moment. Maybe she could find contentment and hope…and a reason to keep getting up every morning. Maybe.

"What about this one?" Caleb asked, coming to a stop. He dropped her hand to point at about eight feet of fairly nice Douglas fir. "That's pretty good, right?"

Sally considered the tree he was indicating and shrugged. "I guess. What about something bigger?"

"Bigger?" He looked at her in surprise. "How much bigger?"

"Oh, about that big around, but maybe twice as tall?"

"*Twice* as tall?"

"Have you not seen the ceiling in Aldo's living room? That space is huge!" The part of the living room that wasn't under the loft soared two stories high.

Caleb looked pained. "So we're looking for a monster? And I'm supposed to drag said monster back to the car by myself? Not to mention hoist it on top of the car? No wonder your pal Aldo elected to stay home. I knew he didn't like me."

Sally laughed. "I'm sure they have people here who can help. Besides, what are you talking about? Of course Aldo likes you! Why on earth would he invite you up here if he didn't?"

Caleb shook his head. "I don't know. I've been asking myself that same question for two days now."

Sally felt her cheeks grow hot. Aldo had invited Caleb for her—she had thought they were all well aware of that. That hadn't been the point she'd been trying to make. "What I meant was, yes, he invited you here because he thought you and I would like it, but he still wouldn't have suggested this if he hadn't wanted to spend some time with you as well."

"That could be, I suppose." Caleb wrapped an arm around her waist and pulled her flush against him. "You know him better than I do, and not that I'm arguing or anything, but the man's a fool. If I were him, I'd want you all to myself. There's no way I'd have invited me up here."

His kiss took her a little by surprise, but it was his words that really shocked her. Did he really not know Aldo was gay? That seemed unlikely. She'd never known Aldo to hide his interests, and given the way he'd been staring at Caleb all through breakfast, he wasn't hiding anything.

Of course, interested or not, if Caleb wasn't gay, Aldo would *not* pursue him. That was something else she knew about her friend—one of the very first things she'd ever learned about him, in fact. Somewhere along the line, someone had hurt him, and ever since then, he did *not* allow himself to fall for people who couldn't return his interest. It was a matter of principle for him, a matter of pride; and it had been an article of faith for Sally. It was how she'd assuaged her guilt all these years whenever she was troubled by the thought that maybe she'd owed it to Aldo, owed it to their friendship, to try harder to resist her feelings for Davis.

On the other hand, maybe she had that backward. Maybe Aldo had felt he owed her. Maybe, in his mind, introducing her to Davis made up for the fact that *he* couldn't return her interest in him. But that was all so long ago. It was water under a bridge—and with Davis's death, the bridge had burned down. There was no way back for any of them now...and maybe no way forward, either.

Depressed by the direction her thoughts were taking, Sally wrapped her arms around Caleb's neck, kissed him harder, and resolved to put the past behind her, at least for one day...or maybe a week. *Life* owed her that, didn't it? One perfect holiday? One week out of time, away from reality, away from the emptiness that had begun to consume her? Next month she'd go back to that, to the drudgery her life had become. She'd go back to muddling through each day, struggling through the murk that seemed to separate each isolated bright spot from the distant next one.

She didn't know what would happen with Caleb after this week. She didn't know what either of them wanted or what either of them was capable of. He had a job and commitments she couldn't even begin to comprehend. After his work here was done, he'd be sent somewhere else, he'd become someone else...how could any relationship survive that?

"So, twice as big, huh?" Caleb asked when they finally came up for air. His smile was unexpectedly tender, but the expression in his eyes was so odd, questioning, faintly sad. It sent tendrils of unease snaking through her happiness. Maybe one perfect week *was* too much to ask for. "Do you even know if Aldo has a tall enough ladder to reach that high? Or enough decorations to fill up a tree that big?"

"Fine," she agreed, rolling her eyes a little. "You

might have a small point there, spoilsport. Maybe just a little bigger?"

* * * *

Aldo was wrapping a thick strand of lighted garland along the railing of the deck when they rolled back into the yard later that day. He stopped what he was doing to stare in disbelief at the tree strapped to the truck's roof. "You couldn't say no to her, could you?" he asked, directing the question to Caleb as he climbed from the cab.

Caleb shrugged and shot a quick glance her way. "What can I say? The lady is very persuasive."

"And you, my friend, are whipped," Aldo replied. "I should've known you couldn't handle her."

"Hey!" Sally shot a mock glare at him. "That's enough of that! Are you just going to stand up there and run your mouth, or are you gonna come help us?"

That brought a grin to Aldo's face. "Ooh, tough words. What do you mean *us* anyway?" he asked teasingly even as he ambled down the stairs, just as ordered. "Don't tell me *you're* planning on lifting that thing down from there? Because that would be a first."

"You're a fine one to talk about being whipped." Caleb gazed pointedly at Aldo. "Seems to me you got your ass down here pretty quick when she told you to."

"Yeah, well, what you call persuasive, I call bossy. Plus I'm not stupid, you know. I've seen her handle a weapon."

Sally rolled her eyes. "That's it; I'm outta here. You boys don't want my help? Well, then, fine. I need to save my hands for my work anyway. So I'll just head on into the house and pour myself a drink, leave all the grunt work for you he-men to do." She nodded toward the single string of lights Aldo had tacked up around the door. "Hey. That's looking good, by the way."

"Thanks." He gave her a wry smile that made her wonder if they weren't both thinking the same thing. It had been sweet of him to make the effort, but if Davis was here, he'd have laughed and called Aldo's handiwork pathetic. Then he'd have spent the rest of the day wrapping the entire cabin in lights.

It took awhile, and the tree must have grown larger on the way here—that was really the only explanation Sally could come up with—because it barely fit through the door. The two men eventually succeeded in maneuvering the tree inside the house, amid much swearing, mostly by Aldo. It looked beautiful, though, when they finally got it set up in front of the big picture window that looked out over the lake. In the meantime Sally had discovered the cozy fire Aldo had lit in the big, stone fireplace and the pitcher of dirty martinis chilling in the fridge.

True to her word, she'd poured herself a drink, took a seat on the couch, and sat back to watch the show. Though she took great pleasure in teasing the men, egging them both on, and even setting them against each other at times, she was actually touched by all of Aldo's little gestures. The martinis were part of a personal tradition that dated back to the first Christmas after the two of them had met, back when their friendship was new and untried.

Back then Sally had still been starry-eyed and hopeful. She'd still believed that Aldo's feelings for her could magically transform into the kind of love she'd wanted from him, that their friendship could develop into something more, something deeper. That was before Davis and heartbreak and several rounds of despair had come between them and, somehow, forged their bonds even stronger.

She guessed it was lucky after all, the way things had worked out for them, because otherwise she would likely have lost both Davis and Aldo by now. And where would that have left her tonight?

After the lights were on the tree, Aldo insisted they stop and eat dinner before the actual decorating could commence. He'd made lasagna—Davis's favorite—and kept the drinks flowing so that, by the time they'd returned to the living room, Sally was feeling buzzed and mellow and only the littlest bit melancholy. She didn't think she was drunk, however, not really, which was why she was caught by surprise when Aldo leaned over the back of the couch where she was seated to kiss her on the cheek and announce that he was turning in for the night.

She looked up at him questioningly. "What, already? No, you can't! We're just getting started."

"Sure I can." He laughed. Then he nodded across the room to where Caleb was still gamely struggling to space the ornaments evenly among the tree's branches. "Besides, it looks like you've got everything well in hand down here. You don't really need my help any more tonight."

Sally wasn't sure whether he was talking about the tree or Caleb. Either way, she felt her cheeks grow warm. She was about to point out that he was being silly, that there was no earthly reason for him to leave, that he should just stay and keep them company awhile longer, when it dawned on her that maybe she was the one being silly—or really obtuse. Maybe he and Caleb had worked this out between them.

Given that she and Caleb had separate rooms, a fact that had, somehow, managed to slip her mind in the last few hours, this was the only way the two of them could actually get some time alone. She'd kind of forgotten about that. Things had been so comfortable this evening with all three of them together, it was almost like old times, almost as though Caleb was slipping automatically into the space left by Davis's absence. That thought sent a cold shiver zinging up her spine. It stabbed at her heart and pierced through the soft, warm fuzziness in her head. She swallowed hard, blinking back the sudden tears in her eyes. Maybe she wasn't as ready to move on as she'd convinced herself the other night. Maybe she should follow Aldo's lead and head to bed herself?

Before she could make good on the thought, however, Caleb wandered over to sit beside her. He took a sip of his coffee, which was heavily laced with spiced rum, if the scent of it was anything to go by. "Everything okay?" he asked, eyeing her curiously.

Her smile felt shaky as she nodded in reply, but it must have satisfied him because he wrapped an arm around her shoulders and pulled her close. She nestled against him and slid a hand up his chest. She wondered if he was hairy or smooth under his shirt and whether she'd ever get the chance to find out.

"You haven't told me what you think about it," he said, nodding at the tree. "That's probably the best I can do, so I hope you like it."

"I do. I think it's beautiful."

"I think you're beautiful." He pressed a quick kiss to her head, then pulled back to look at her. "Seriously, you looked like an angel tonight, or something even more magical. I was noticing earlier, when we were trimming the tree. Your hair…it was like fire and ice, shimmering with the lights from the tree."

Sally shrugged. "It's a thermotropic, reflective hair dye." It was her one indulgence, her one concession to being a girlie girl. Her naturally fair hair had always struck her as boring and plain.

"I kept wanting to touch it, to see if it would be cold or hot. I kept wanting to touch you too." He grinned suddenly. "I wanted to pinch you and see if you're real or just a dream."

"P-pinch…*me*?" The words caught in her throat. Even with the martinis, she knew that was backward, knew it was himself he should have been pinching, unless that wasn't what he meant at all. Her breath hitched. Unless he meant something entirely different. And just like that, just that quickly, memories that had lain trapped for months in the depths of her subconscious swirled up to float free on the surface of her mind. Memories of strong hands that knew just how she liked to be touched, how much pain or pressure to apply and where and when…

From somewhere deep inside, hunger flared, bringing

a rush of need that trembled through her. Oh, to be touched like that again. She needed it. Now. Right now…

"What do you mean?" she asked as the heat rose in her cheeks. "Pinch me where?"

"What?" Caleb glanced curiously at her; then his eyes widened. "Oh, I see." A wicked smile lit up his face. "You'd like that, would you?" His voice was low; it vibrated within her, in that same, deep place where desire resided, where all her darkest fantasies dwelled. She bit her lip.

"C'mon, Sally, talk to me," Caleb said when the silence dragged on a little too long. "Tell me what you're thinking. I don't want to make another mistake like I did the other night, assuming I knew what was in your head. Tell me what you want."

Tell him what she wanted? No, she couldn't. She'd die of embarrassment. It wasn't exactly visions of sugarplums dancing in her head right now; it was something darker, more scary, and so much hotter than that. She and Davis had been together years before she'd dared to even hint at it.

Caleb's eyes were hot on her as he carefully reached out and took the glass from her hand. After placing her glass and his coffee on the coffee table, he twisted around on the couch so he could face her.

"Okay, let's try something then," he suggested. His hands were warm as they lightly caged her head, his lips brushed gently against hers, and the spicy taste of the coffee he'd been drinking was just as intriguing as she'd hoped. She closed her eyes, lulled by the sweetness and the spice, by the softness of his kiss. It was nice, warm, and safe…maybe a little too safe. Then his touch turned firm.

His hands smoothed over her shoulders and down her arms, gently urging her hands behind her, causing her back to arch. Her nipples swelled to tight peaks. Sweet, liquid heat flowed through her, and just like that, she was caught.

The look in his eyes as he pulled back to gaze at her said he knew it too. "Yeah, okay. That's what I thought. You like this, don't you?"

Her breath faltered. Light-headed, she sat frozen in her need, trying not to whimper, trying not to squirm. Trying not to beg for one touch. Just one touch. *I need, I need... No, damn it. Not just one touch. Everything. I need you to make me give you everything. Make me beg for it. Now.*

"Well? Don't you?" The question demanded an answer. It demanded she speak and left no room for there to be any other answer save one.

"Yes." The word stumbled out eagerly on a breathy little sigh. Between the pounding of her heart and the stuttering of her breath, she wouldn't have even been sure she'd spoken it aloud if it weren't for the flare of heat and need and triumph in his eyes. *Oh yes.*

"Okay, good. At least now I know we're on the same page."

He pressed her wrists together a little more firmly than before, tightening his grip so he could hold her with one hand, so that his other hand was free to slip under the front of her sweater. Soft fingers glided up her abdomen. Her muscles rippled in response.

"So, did Aldo go to bed already?" Caleb asked in a voice so close to conversational she was momentarily thrown.

"Yeah, a...a couple of minutes ago."

"That was considerate of him, I guess." Caleb's gaze met hers. His lips curved upward in another knowing smile. "Or was it? Are you sure he isn't planning on coming back down again?"

"Mm-mm. I don't think so."

"No?"

His eyes were still hot on hers as his hand moved higher, under her shirt, over her bra. *Not enough.* Her sex clenched as his fingers brushed lightly across her nipples, the hard little points that longed for his touch. *Not enough. Harder!*

"Do you want him to?"

His words caught her by surprise. A slight frown furrowed her brow. She didn't want to talk, didn't want to think. She just wanted to feel.

"Do you want him to come back down and catch me playing with you like this?" Caleb elaborated.

She answered with a shrug. She didn't know what she wanted anymore where Aldo was concerned. It had been years since she'd thought about it, years since it had even mattered.

"What would he do, do you think? Would he sit down and watch, just let me have my way with you? Maybe he'd offer suggestions. Maybe he'd touch himself. Would it turn you on if he did? Or is that not enough? Would you want him to join us?"

She moved restlessly against his hand, too distracted by the sudden flood of images in her mind to sit still any longer. She was rewarded with a stern pinch that had her sucking in a quick, startled breath. Her toes curled. Her pussy clenched. She writhed shamelessly in his grasp, earning herself a flurry of increasingly hard little tugs and twists that left her feeling molten. *Oh yeah...*

Just as suddenly as it had started, the barrage stopped. "Answer the question," Caleb murmured, lightly brushing his fingers across her sensitized flesh. There was the faintest hint of a threat in his voice, but it was enough.

"More." The word forced its way past her lips on a wave of melting, aching need. "Oh, please more."

"Wrong answer." Caleb used the hand that held her wrists to urge her up onto her knees, while his other hand pushed her sweater higher. He took her nipple in his mouth, then sucked her through the thin lace of her bra, eliciting a helpless moan. Then he stopped and looked up at her curiously. "Or maybe it was just the wrong question. More as in more of *this*." He bit gently on her nipple once again. "Or more as in, 'let's go upstairs and drag that lazy ass out of bed already'?"

Sally shook her head. "This." It would do no good to

even think about anything else. She couldn't even make that work as a fantasy. Aldo didn't play that way. At best he'd gaze pityingly at her and suggest she lay off the martinis in the future. "Just this."

"All right," Caleb agreed. He let her sweater drop and started unfastening her jeans. "Can't argue with that. Still, you can't blame a guy for trying, either."

It took Caleb a minute or so to undo her pants one-handed. Sally's heart was thundering with anticipation. It was all she could do to keep from squirming, all she could do to keep from wrenching her hands free and doing it herself. She resisted—but only because she didn't want him to stop, didn't want to give him any excuse to end this game.

Finally, finally he got them open and shoved partly down. Then he slid his hand between her legs and inside her panties to cup her mound, calling her attention to the bareness there. Shaving had become such a habit, she had no idea why she'd kept it up these past few months other than a refusal to accept there was no longer a reason for it. She jerked as his fingers slipped lower, brushing over her clit, sending fire to lick through her veins. It was all she could do to keep from rocking her hips and grinding hard against his hand. Her breath stuttered with the effort to hold still.

Caleb groaned softly. "Oh yeah. You're so hot for me, sweet baby. Aren't you?" He rubbed slowly, back and forth. "Hot and so, so wet."

Sally nodded, nibbling at her bottom lip. *More. Give me more.* As though in answer to her silent plea, on his next stroke Caleb slid one finger deep inside her. Her breath caught on a gasp. *There. Right there.* That was exactly where she wanted him.

"Here's what I think we're gonna do," Caleb said, using the same conversational tone he'd used before. It was so at odds with what his hand was doing—pulling out, stroking deep, spreading wetness all around—that it sent delicious tingles rushing through her. It made everything she was feeling seem so much more wicked. "I want to take you just like this. Right here on the couch, because I think you like that idea. I'm going to let you ride my fingers, let you rub off on my hand. I want to watch you come, feel you when you come apart. Then I'm gonna roll you over and fuck you senseless. But first..." He pulled his hand from her pants, and she had to stifle a cry of disappointment. *No, don't stop. Where are you going?* But then he grabbed the hem of her sweater, and as his intentions became clear, her blood surged faster. He wasn't going anywhere, but what he was doing was going to drive her right out of her fucking mind.

She swallowed a sob as excitement thrummed through her. Caleb shoved her sweater up and over her head until it was bunched at the back of her neck and tight across the front of her shoulders. She felt like she was wearing a harness. One that restricted her movements, showcased her breasts, and gave him all the access he could ever need. The sweater was probably going to be ruined after this, stretched hopelessly out of shape. She couldn't care less.

Next he lowered the cups of her bra. "I want to watch 'em bounce," he explained with an evil grin that left her with no doubt he knew exactly the effect his words and his actions were having on her. "Plus this way you're giving me something to entertain myself with while you work your hot little pussy for me. And this..." His fingers traced lazy, wet circles around each of her nipples. "This will make them taste extra nice."

Again it took her a moment to connect the dots. Those were the same fingers that had just been inside her. They were wet with her juices. The thought left her light-headed. Her nipples hardened even more. Caleb's grin widened. "Oh, I guess you like that too." He lifted his hand to her face and painted over her lips before sliding his finger between them. "What about this?"

She groaned impatiently, sucking at his finger, unable to keep from squirming. If he didn't take her soon, she was going to jump him. "C'mon..."

"Uh-uh." He tapped lightly on her nose. "None of

that. No fussing allowed. Just say, 'yes, Caleb' whenever I ask you a question. That's all I want to hear from you tonight. But I want you to say my name like you do Aldo's, all sweet and soft like you'd do anything for him."

Sally had no idea what he was talking about, but she tried her best. "Caleb," she murmured softly. "Yesss."

"Close enough," he said as he took the fingers that had just been in her mouth into his own.

She chewed on her lip again, but the slight salt taste that lingered there was almost more than she could take. Her pussy clenched, and she tried to press her legs together to relieve the pressure. "Caleb…"

"Am I gonna regret telling you how much I love that?" he asked, chuckling softly as he finally slipped his hand between her legs once again. "Keep talking like that and you're gonna make me want to do whatever you want too."

Which would only be fair, Sally thought, giving a heartfelt moan as his fingers once again slid across her clit, since that's how she was feeling right now about him.

"All right, come on." Caleb scooted a little closer. He took one nipple between his teeth and teased just the tip of it with his tongue. Sensation shivered through her. "This is what you've been asking for, isn't it?" he pulled off to ask. "Well? Let me hear it."

Sally blinked in confusion, her mind too lust fogged, at first, to respond. "Yes, Caleb," she gasped when he threatened to withdraw his hand. "Yes yes."

"Right. So then this is your chance." He urged her into motion with the hand at her back. "No more talking, just give it all up for me like a good girl." She clenched her hands tighter until she could feel the points of her nails digging into her palms. Then she began to move, hesitant at first, then increasingly harder, loving the tug on her nipples as she moved away, loving the way his finger slid deeper inside when she rolled in close.

"I love how wet you are right now," he murmured. "I

want to spread all that lovely sweet juice around, from your pussy to your ass, all over, everywhere. Wanna get you all nice and slick, inside and out. Then I'm gonna fuck you there too."

Just for an instant Sally's rhythm faltered. Her medical training surged to the fore. Words like *bacterial infection* and *cross contamination* tumbled around in her brain, threatening to pull her out of the moment. Damn it all, it was just talk, a fantasy. He wasn't actually doing anything like that. Still she shook her head.

"No?" Caleb looked at her in surprise. "Ah, well, we'll work up to that later then." He leaned in to tease one swollen nipple again, and sizzling heat all but consumed her. "But I promise," he whispered, his breath cool against her wet skin. "When you're ready, you're gonna love it."

She could easily believe that. She'd love it right now, but they had to be safe, they had to be smart about it.

"C'mon, faster," Caleb urged. "Fuck my hand. Nice and hard now." He twisted his hand so that his thumb slid inside her, thick and blunt. She keened softly. The tips of his fingers brushed teasingly over her anus, and all her muscles threatened to tighten and seize. Once again her rhythm faltered. Once again his hand prodded at her back; this time he tugged at her sweater as well. Her breasts jutted forward. "Don't stop." The words were accompanied by a quick nip at her breast. "Don't you dare stop until I tell you." His voice was a low growl, an outright order. A sob left her lips as she rocked harder, even despite the tremors racing up her legs. Her clit bumped against the heel of his hand with every stroke. Her bare breasts jiggled in place. She felt naked and exposed, vulnerable and wanton, both her mind and her body totally on display. He knew just what she was, just what she wanted. She couldn't get over that fact. She wasn't even sure how it was possible for anyone to know someone else so intimately in so short a time. The knowledge that he did, that he had put his finger so unerringly on the pulse of her desires, broke her open. Fire swept through her veins, and she came hard, her body jolted by the shock waves.

She was still coming when he lifted and turned her. She felt the cushions at her back as he laid her on the couch and came down on top of her, a warm, heavy weight that chased away the sudden chill and kept her feeling safe and protected. "So hot," he murmured as he shoved her pants out of the way and started in on his own. "So fucking hot. Gotta have you now."

"Yes, Caleb," she said, just to watch his response, see how he'd react to the sound of her voice, thick and saturated with sated lust.

He reacted with a shudder. His eyes dilated, went black with heat. His voice rumbled from his chest. "Oh fuck. I need a condom. Now."

As he twisted his body around to reach for his pants, Sally felt a frown begin to form. *A condom? Why would he... Oh.*

It was such a small thing, the kind of thing she should have thought of herself, but like the tiniest crack will sometimes expand and bring the whole wall down, that one word opened a chasm at her feet. Big. Black. Endless.

Davis was dead.

It had been years since she'd thought of condoms, years since she'd had any need for them. But those days were gone now. And so was her husband.

She turned her head to the side as a sob welled up her throat. Caleb twisted back around to face her. "Sally? What's wrong?" The worried note in his voice undid her. He was concerned about her. She could hear it. Even now, his first thought was for her. How had she gotten so lucky? Her eyes filled with tears. She shook her head, unable to answer, sobs coming faster now. "Shit."

In a flash he had her off her back and in his arms, cradled on his lap. She clung to him helplessly.

"Please, don't cry. What is it, baby? What'd I do?"

Sally shook her head. "Not you," she blurted between sobs. "No no. Not you. D-Davis."

"Your husband? Oh." And that was the last he said for a while. He tugged her clothes back into place, then rocked her gently, wiping at her tears and waiting out the storm.

"S-s-sorry," she stuttered when her grief had worn itself out. She tried to pull away, but he held her tight.

"Nothing to be sorry about." He gazed curiously at her. "So is this your first time with anyone since…?"

Sally nodded, blinking back a fresh fall of tears. She hadn't realized it would be so hard to let go. She should have known better.

"Ah." His voice sounded so sad. "I guess it was a little too soon, huh?"

Sally shook her head. "I don't think it's that. It just hit me all of a sudden, the fact that he's gone. Maybe because it's Christmas Eve. He always loved the holidays so much."

"Maybe my coming up here this week was a bad idea."

She shook her head again. "No. Don't think that. Please. I wanted you here. I still do. It's just…tonight. It's harder than I thought it would be, and I don't…I don't think I can do this right now."

"I understand." He was quiet for a moment, then asked, "So let me ask you something. The other night, if I hadn't left, would tonight have been easier for you? If we were lovers before now, I mean. Or would the same thing have happened either way?"

Sally stared, stricken, at him. "I'm not punishing you for that. Please don't think that's what this is about."

"I don't." Caleb smiled gently. "That's not what I meant. I'm just trying to put things in perspective, figure out what to do next. I mean, maybe the other night was just a missed opportunity, or maybe it was the *only* opportunity. If I've been pushing you too hard, if you need more time, I could catch the first bus out of here tomorrow. I'm sure something'll be running, even with the holiday."

"No, please don't do that. If anything, having you

here makes it easier. Aldo and I…we have so many memories of Davis. Sometimes they won't leave me alone."

"Well, that's okay too, you know. Nothing wrong with that. Memories are precious. Believe me. That's something I know a little bit about. You want to hold on to them as long as you can."

"I guess. Maybe." Sally rested her head against Caleb's shoulder. She wasn't worried about forgetting Davis; she knew she never could. She treasured the memories they'd made, the life they'd built together. She hadn't wanted any of it to end, but it had all the same. If she ever wanted to heal, if she wanted to move on and maybe build something new, either alone or with someone else, she couldn't stay where she was. The past was a ghost, an empty shell; it was no longer capable of sustaining life. She had to accept that and find some way to close the door on her memories, or her grief would kill her. "Please don't leave yet. I really want you to stay through the next week like we planned."

"All right, if you're sure."

"I am."

Caleb sighed. "Still, I think we should call it a night."

Sally nodded. "I think you're right." She stood up reluctantly. Her lonely room, her empty bed had never seemed less enticing, but she'd never convince Caleb she wanted to move on if she kept dissolving into tears, and she strongly suspected more tears were on their way. "Merry Christmas," she said as she leaned down and kissed him on the cheek. "And thank you."

* * * *

Sally made short work of getting ready for bed, but sleep did not come easily. Thoughts of Davis kept intruding. All she could think about as she lay in the empty bed was the last time they'd made love…

It had been early morning, just a few days before his death. He'd woken her in the manner she loved most, with his lips on her neck. His morning beard had rasped her sensitive skin. He'd spooned her from behind, his arms wrapped tight around her. One curved around her rib cage, his hand cupping her breast, fingers toying with her nipple. The other extended over her hip, slipping between her legs, long fingers lightly brushing her clit. She'd moaned and arched against him, and his touch had grown more demanding.

"Open." His voice, husky and low, turned her liquid. She did so willingly. She lifted her top leg and then slid it back until it rested on his. She hooked her foot beneath his calf, and he shifted his leg back, drawing her leg with it, opening her even wider to his touch. "Yeah, like that," he murmured approvingly. He slipped one finger inside her. "So wet." He pulled out, spreading her moisture over her lower lips, circling her clit with it. "You're so wet for me, baby."

His other hand was on her throat now, his thumb urging her chin higher. He nuzzled her ear. "I wish I had all day to spend with you. If I had the time, I'd drive you so crazy. I'd tease you till you begged for it..."

If she'd known it would be the last time, she'd have insisted on it. She'd have drawn it out, made it last longer, made it last hours; she'd have spent the whole day in bed with him—just like he'd said, the way they'd done when they were first married. She'd have spent less time being pleasured and more time pleasuring him. But she hadn't known. All those moments lost, all that time wasted. It was too late now for her and Davis; she'd never know that love again. But she would know someone's love. And she'd never waste another chance.

Chapter Seven

The sound of Sally's laughter, so sexy and low, worked its way into Caleb's dreams. Today was Christmas, he remembered as he opened his eyes, surprised to find her lying naked beside him. What was she doing in his bed? He distinctly remembered parting company with her last night, kissing her one last time at the door of her room, and wishing her a merry Christmas.

Yet here she was, watching him with a mischievous gleam in her eyes and her lips stretched wide around what had to be the most phallic-looking candy cane in the whole world. He had never yet found a reason to question what a beautiful, naked woman with an obvious oral fixation should be doing in his bed—especially not first thing in the morning—and he saw no reason to start now.

"Where'd you get that thing?" he asked instead, his cock hardening almost painfully at the sight of her sliding the hard candy in and out of her mouth.

"Mm. It's good," she said in reply, although how she managed to enunciate so clearly was yet another mystery. "Really, really good. You ought to try it."

"Hey, let me have some of that," Aldo said as he reached over Caleb's shoulder to take the candy from Sally's hand.

Caleb twisted around to look. As he suspected, Aldo was equally naked and equally breathtaking. "Nash, what are you doing here?" he demanded, all the same trying desperately to hang on to the memory of anger, to the memory of—again, distinctly—not liking the man, but it was a lost cause. Maybe he should just man up. Maybe it was time to admit to the attraction he was feeling. As Aldo's tongue swiped lazily, up and down along the length of the sugar shaft and Caleb's personal candy cane jerked impatiently, longing for its turn, he could at least admit this much: He would not be kicking Aldo out of his bed this morning either. If he wanted to be here right now, fine. Caleb could go back to hating him later.

"Here. Taste this one." Sally was smiling wider now as she held the candy teasingly close to Caleb's face.

Caleb blinked in surprise. He hadn't seen her retrieve the candy from Aldo, but obviously she must have done so at some point. He didn't care. He'd had enough foreplay. "I'd rather taste you," Caleb said as he reached for her, but Aldo tackled him from behind, holding him close, nuzzling against his neck.

"Not so fast," Aldo murmured, his breath warm against Caleb's cheek, his voice echoing oddly. "You have to choose. Which is it gonna be? Pick one or the other. You can't have us both."

"Don't say that." Panic tightened Caleb's chest to the point where it was hard to breathe. There was an all too familiar note of finality in Aldo's voice. Caleb couldn't recall when he'd heard it before, but he simply couldn't accept that Aldo meant it. "Please don't say that. Don't make me choose between you. I can't!"

"You mean you won't." Aldo growled as he shoved Caleb away from him. "Same as always. Fine, then. That's your choice. Live with it."

"No, wait." Tears sprang suddenly into Caleb's eyes. Some inconsolable heartache tore through his chest. He turned to plead with him, but Aldo was already gone.

"Oh, Caleb." Sally shook her head sadly at him. "Don't you get it? Choosing not to choose is still choosing, you know. If you don't choose something, you'll always end up with nothing."

"No. Please." Nothing was what he had now; he hadn't expected a lifetime of it. He reached for her once again—and promptly woke up.

The voices continued, however, still conversational, sounding no farther away than before, only now that he was awake, he recognized them as filtering in from the kitchen rather than originating here in his room. He felt the pain in his chest recede. It was only a dream.

There were several obvious advantages to having been kitted out with so-called superhearing, but imagining that a conversation taking place several rooms away had anything to do with you wasn't one of them. Especially not when it sparked a dream like that one.

What had that been about? he wondered as he rolled over in bed and fingered his achingly full shaft. Obviously some parts of him hadn't found the dream all that upsetting. Aldo's mouth—that's what his cock was choosing to remember right now. Which was just confusing as hell.

Shouldn't it be Sally making him feel frustrated and unsatisfied this morning? Or had jerking off in bed last night while his mind replayed every moment of their scene on the couch, of her coming apart in his hands, put that puppy to rest?

Maybe Aldo reminded him of someone he used to know? Obviously they'd both served time in the military. He'd probably met lots of men with similar manners or mannerisms. Hell, maybe they'd even known each other, once upon a time. It wasn't impossible, just really, really, massively far-fetched. Not that they'd ever know. His memories were gone, and according to what he'd overheard in the hospital once when they'd thought his ears weren't functioning, his own mother wouldn't recognize him now. Assuming she was still alive.

Another pang tightened his chest, startling him with its intensity. It would be kind of nice to know what he'd walked away from or whether there was anyone out there somewhere who was maybe still waiting for him. He'd been assured that the program only accepted applicants with no family ties, but it certainly wouldn't surprise him to learn that they'd lied...or maybe he'd lied to them. Who knew? It could've happened like that.

He couldn't think about that now, however. He tightened his grasp on his cock and stroked, pushing those thoughts and worries far to the back of his mind. Just like the other night, when he was alone in the woods, the image that sprang into his mind was of Aldo. He imagined himself back in the dream that had just ended. Only this time it didn't end there…

* * * *

"You made your choice." Aldo growled as he shoved Caleb away. "Live with it." As he turned to leave, Caleb grabbed him by the shoulders and wrestled him down onto the bed.

"No." Caleb shoved Aldo facedown and clambered on top of him. "Don't you walk away from me. Don't you do it. Not again. You're mine—remember? You said it yourself, damn it. You fucking swore to it."

"Not anymore." Aldo shook his head. "I can't keep doing this with you, Kay. It's over." His voice sounded so serious, like he really might mean it this time, but the way his body shuddered under Caleb's told a far different story.

"C'mon, baby," he pleaded, his body pressing harder on Aldo's, his lips so close to the other man's ear he could have nibbled on it. "Don't do this to us. We can work it out. Please."

"How?" Aldo's voice cracked with anger, but Caleb didn't miss the fact that Aldo's body was no longer fighting him. "How we gonna work it out this time? Same way as always, with more of your lies?"

"I never lied to you," Caleb whispered fiercely even as he used his legs to force Aldo's farther apart. He slid his fingers between them, caressing, teasing, featherlight touches trailing over the other man's balls, his taint, his tightly closed hole. "I've been straight with you from the start—you know that."

"Straight. Right." Aldo's voice held its bitter, mocking edge, even as his entrance relaxed, even as his breath hitched and his fists curled tighter. "That's what you'd like to think, right? Straight as in, you like girls? Yeah, sure. Girls and my gay ass, apparently. Lucky me." He bucked his hips and growled again. "Stop, damn it. I'm not falling for this bullshit anymore."

"Shh," Caleb soothed. He bit softly on Aldo's shoulder. "You know that's not what I'm saying." There'd been other men, they'd just all been before the two of them had gotten together. How the hell Aldo couldn't see that as a good thing was a mystery Caleb had given up trying to solve. Apparently the fact that he'd never even been tempted to cheat on Al with another guy was winning him no points with his lover—all he fucking cared about were the women. "You know how I feel about you, baby. You know." And okay, maybe that was a lie—but it was just a small one. Because sometimes Caleb himself wasn't sure how he felt. Could be Aldo was right. Could be the fact that Caleb couldn't give Aldo what he needed meant that what he felt for the other man wasn't really love. It felt like it, though. "Need you," he groaned in his lover's ear. "Please, baby…"

"Need. You. Too." Aldo ground the three words out as he bowed his head, shoulders sagging in defeat. He bent one leg, pulling it up toward his chest, opening himself for Caleb. "You fucking bastard. I need you too."

Less than a minute later, Caleb slid home, feeling as grateful as if he'd just dodged a bullet. *Love you, babe.* The words filled Caleb's head, but he kept his mouth shut and concentrated on angling his hips to nail Aldo's gland again and again. That he could do. As for words? He was pretty damn sure they were the last thing Aldo wanted right now, especially not from the fucking bastard who was taking his ass. But it felt true, all the same. *Love you. Love you. Love you…*

* * * *

Caleb groaned. He reached for the tissues just in time. He was sweating like he'd just run a race. Where were all these weird fantasies coming from? True, this one had started out as a dream, and dreams were frequently weird, but still.

Voices were still murmuring in the kitchen. Judging by the other noises that accompanied them, Caleb deduced that his housemates were breakfasting without him. The thought left him feeling shut out and—something else that was unusual for him—lonely. All these strange sensations and strong emotions just weren't right. He wondered if his neural hardware was malfunctioning again.

He knew his implants were capable of interfering with his body's natural ability to process pain signals, but that was something he could turn on and off at will. What of his brain's ability to experience negative or undesirable emotions? Might that have been suppressed as well? He'd been considering the possibility for a while. Judging from what he'd observed, most "normals" had emotions that were a lot more volatile than his own. And a lot more like the ones he was feeling now, the ones he'd been feeling for the better part of the last month.

It wouldn't surprise him to learn that his normal responses had been dulled down—for his own good. It made good sense for that to be the case. Why allow a soldier to become paralyzed by fear if you didn't need to? Why allow him to feel loss if doing so would only jeopardize his mission? The ability to form close, interpersonal bonds might be useful if he were working as part of a team, but that hadn't been a part of Caleb's reality for quite a while.

Until this mission, until these last several weeks, Caleb had had no trouble keeping his work and his personal life separate—mostly because he hadn't had a personal life to speak of. He hadn't needed one. He sure as hell hadn't missed one. This morning, he had to admit, that was no longer true. It hadn't been true in a while.

* * * *

Sally and Aldo were seated at the kitchen table when Caleb joined them there. His initial reaction was disappointment. They looked so comfortable with each other, so content. He almost hated to interrupt the pretty picture they made—like an illustration for domestic bliss. Delicious fragrances wafted through the air, but the food that had produced them was nowhere in sight. There remained nothing edible on the table other than some oranges, a plate of Christmas cookies, and two half-empty mugs of coffee. Maybe it was too much for Caleb to expect to be included in every activity, every meal, maybe he was nothing but an afterthought—an intruder, no matter how much Sally insisted otherwise, but couldn't they at least have saved him something?

Aldo glanced up just then and saw him. "Well, it's about time you decided to join us," he said as he got to his feet. He grabbed the coffee mugs and headed toward the stove. "I was starting to think you'd never get up. And she"—he nodded at Sally—"wouldn't let me wake you."

Sally had turned in her seat to smile at Caleb. Now she rolled her eyes. "It's a holiday, Aldo. Stop fussing. Show some holiday cheer. Besides, not everyone is as perky as you in the morning."

"I am *not* perky," Aldo insisted. "I am *never* perky, damn it, and I am especially not perky before breakfast."

Caleb couldn't help sympathizing. He wouldn't ever want to be described as perky either. He crossed to Sally's side and bent down to kiss her. Her lips were warm and soft and faintly sugary. "Mm. Sweet," he murmured, then kissed her again. "Good morning."

"Merry Christmas," she answered softly. Then she pulled back and indicated the plate on the table. "It's the cookies that're sweet. Try one—they're still warm. Aldo's outdone himself this year."

Caleb's eyebrows rose. "You didn't just bake these this morning, did you?"

Aldo shrugged. "I had time on my hands. It was something to do."

The cookies looked professional. Caleb would have bet money they'd come from a bakery. He was sure they were delicious, but his idea of breakfast involved something a little more substantial. He glanced at the other man curiously. "You really like this cooking thing, huh?"

"Like I said, it was something to do."

Sally rolled her eyes again. "That means yes," she said, smiling at Caleb again. She reached for his hand and gave it a little tug. "Come and sit down. We're about to have breakfast."

Caleb's mood brightened instantly. "You didn't eat yet? I thought you went ahead and ate without me."

Aldo snorted in disgust. "Oh, now there's an idea. Why didn't I think of that?"

"Caleb," Sally murmured in chiding tones. "Of course we didn't. That would've been rude."

"Thank you." Caleb leaned in and kissed her again. His ears had detected the slightest hint of a caress in Sally's voice as she said his name. Warmth blossomed in his chest. As he'd told her last night, he'd do pretty much anything to keep that lilt in her voice.

"Help yourself to coffee if you want," Aldo told him as he returned to the table carrying the two mugs he'd refilled and some kind of egg dish he'd retrieved from the oven.

Caleb nodded. "Okay, thanks." Was it just his imagination, or was the expression on Aldo's face this morning extra frosty? He felt his hackles rise and willed them back down. He didn't want to be mad this morning. He was getting tired of walking around angry all the time. Of course, he didn't want to be attracted to the other man all the time either. He took a deep breath and tried for a smile. "What's that you got there? It looks good."

"It's a frittata," Aldo answered in clipped, disinterested tones.

"It's not *just* a frittata," Sally corrected. "It's a *delicious* frittata. He makes it every year, just for Christmas—see all the red and green bits?"

Aldo sighed. "They're called peppers, honey. Red and green bell peppers."

Sally laughed. Caleb loved the teasing note in her voice as she said, "You're so picky this morning. What does it matter anyway? You both knew what I meant."

"Well, let's see," Aldo answered. "When you perform

a surgery, do you refer to the specific body part you're operating on at all? Or do you just point and say, 'Let's cut out that bit there'?"

Sally shook her head. "Caleb, honey, he's picking on me. Tell the mean, old detective how professional I am."

There it was again, that soft little note in her voice. He could get seriously addicted to that. "Always." Caleb smiled and poured himself some coffee. "She uses all the big words too. She's probably just dumbing things down now so you can follow along."

"Oh, I'm so sure." Aldo rolled his eyes. "You can manage bigger words than 'bit'? You have no idea how relieved I am." Frowning at his plate, Aldo added, "And for the record, I make no claims for the quality of this dish. It's highly unlikely it will be delicious this year. I'm guessing inedible will be closer to the mark, given how long I was forced to keep it in the warmer—through no fault of my own, I might add."

Sally laughed again. "Look at you. You're such a kitchen diva this morning! What's up with that, anyway? You know how awesome you are. Who're you trying to impress?"

From across the room, Caleb watched them enviously, marveling at how amazing they were together. Did they even realize it? And did either of them have any idea how much they were turning him on right now—with their smiles and their glances, their playful banter? Aldo by himself, when it was just the two of them, still had a tendency to piss Caleb off, but put him together with Sally? Totally different dynamic. Every eye roll, every smile had Caleb aching to be a part of it, to laugh and play together like that. To laugh and play together like that in bed, all three of them—oh yeah, that's just what he needed.

It was what Sally needed too, unless he missed his guess. His ears were sensitive enough that he'd heard the way her pulse picked up when he'd mentioned it last night. Hearts don't lie, and given how fast hers was pounding, she'd have liked it a lot if Aldo had joined them. At least in the beginning. Later, when she was crying—yeah, not so much then. That had been a big concern for Caleb, as well. He was sure he'd heard Aldo moving around upstairs at that point too—and had wondered if he was thinking of storming downstairs and making good on his earlier threats to castrate Caleb. He'd been relieved when they'd all made it into their respective beds unscathed. Maybe that was the reason for Aldo's coldness toward him this morning? Hopefully he'd get over it. Hopefully Caleb wouldn't have to worry about having his food poisoned.

"C'mon, Caleb." Sally flashed her warm smile his way. "Let's eat!"

There was a word for what the two of them had, although he couldn't think what it was. Whatever it was, it was something Caleb didn't have. Maybe later, after his malfunctioning neurotransmitters were repaired, he wouldn't care. For now, however, even without knowing exactly what it was, he knew he missed it.

"When are we going to open presents?" Sally asked toward the end of breakfast. The frittata was gone by that point, as were most of the cookies.

Aldo chuckled. "How about right now? Is that soon enough for you? Then afterward I was thinking we could go for a hike in the woods. It's a beautiful day, and it'll give us a chance to work up an appetite for dinner."

Caleb suppressed a sigh. He had no presents for anyone, not that he expected to get any in return. And a walk in the woods? Through the snow? In street shoes? Yeah, not happening. "Good idea. Why don't you two go and do that. Meanwhile I'll stay here and clear away the dishes and stuff."

"Are you sure you don't want to come with us?" Sally asked, glancing at him uncertainly.

Aldo looked him over, his glance piercing and still too cool. "If it's gear you're worried about, there are several pairs of boots in the closet. I'm sure we can find something that will fit."

Caleb's eyebrows rose. "All right then, I will. Thanks."

"Good. Now, gifts." Aldo looked at Sally. "You want to do that here?"

She nodded and patted the empty chair beside her, which wasn't completely empty after all. Caleb noted the festive packages with a sinking heart. Part of him really wanted one of them to be for him. It wasn't his fault he was failing so spectacularly at this whole holiday thing; he had no memories of how it was supposed to be done.

"All right, hold on," Aldo said. He got to his feet and headed for the door. "I'll be right back." When he returned, carrying two small boxes, Caleb's eyebrows rose once again, even higher than before, especially when Aldo slid one of the boxes toward him.

"Thanks," he said once again. It was beginning to feel like that was the only word he knew this morning.

"Here. Open mine first," Sally insisted. She'd given Aldo some hopelessly complicated kitchen appliance that—apparently—was the best thing he'd ever received if the smile on his face when he opened the box was anything to go by.

"I had no idea what to get you," Sally told Caleb while he was unwrapping the box she'd handed him, which held an expensive-looking bottle of brandy. "But I figured this was something you wouldn't be able to buy for yourself. I hope you like it."

"Thank you." Again with the word! "This is perfect." Caleb had no idea if he'd ever even tasted brandy. As of this moment, however, it was his new favorite drink.

Next Sally opened Aldo's gift and laughed in delight. She held up the two tickets the box contained, eyes sparkling as she smiled at Aldo. "Really? You're coming with me?"

He shrugged. "That's what you said you wanted, right? But hey, if there's someone else you'd rather take to the opera with you, go right ahead."

"Oh, no way." Sally shook her head. "You're my arm candy for the night, and that's that. You know there's no one else who wears a tuxedo as well as you do."

"This is very true," Aldo replied, smiling smugly back at her. "I certainly can't argue with that." Then he turned toward Caleb and nodded at the box on the table. "Well? Aren't you going to open it?"

Caleb reached for the box, doing his best to hide his annoyance. There'd been an unmistakable gleam of triumph in Aldo's eyes just now. A look that said all too clearly that he knew exactly what was on Caleb's mind, that he knew Caleb wasn't sure which part annoyed him more, the fact that Sally clearly preferred the sight of Aldo in a tux or the fact that Caleb was secretly in agreement with her. Aldo had looked damned amazing at the party the other night.

Then Caleb opened the box. He felt his face—all the way to the tips of his ears—grow warm. The box contained a scarf. Unless he was greatly mistaken, it was the very one he'd taken from Aldo the other night.

"You seemed to like it," Aldo said pointedly and with considerable smugness.

Caleb cleared his throat. "Yeah. Thanks, man." For a moment Caleb actually considered telling Aldo the truth; what he liked most about the scarf was how it smelled like Aldo. It was almost worth it, to see the surprise in the other man's expression, but fuck that. The cocky bastard certainly didn't need any more of an ego boost. Instead Caleb shot an apologetic glance at Sally. "I'm sorry I didn't think to get anything for either of you."

"Well, you couldn't know you were coming up here," Sally pointed out—completely ignoring the fact that he'd had just as much advance warning as she had.

"Don't sweat it." Aldo rose to his feet once more and stretched languidly, his mocking smile still in place. "Just clear away the dishes for the rest of the week and we'll call it even."

* * * *

As promised, the weather was perfect. The air was crisp and smelled like pine—a warm and unexpectedly sensual fragrance that affected Caleb so strongly he had to repeatedly adjust himself. He supposed it could be the company that was heightening the effect. The woman with whom he was holding hands. The owner of the jacket he was once again wearing—and whose musky scent seemed to blend perfectly with the surrounding fragrances.

Caleb glanced around, hoping to distract himself. There was certainly no dearth of appealing scenery—when he managed to tear his gaze away from his appealing companions. The sky was the color of well-worn jeans. The trees and rocks looked like they'd been dusted with mounds of powdered sugar. As for the lake, glistening far below their trail…well, that didn't even look like water. It looked more like…like emeralds and sapphires, all melted and swirled together.

"Yeah, that's original," Aldo had grumbled when Caleb mentioned it. "Why'd you think they called it Emerald Bay? You're not the first person to think that, you know."

Caleb bit back his response. He wanted to ask Aldo about that stick he'd shoved up his ass. If Sally hadn't been there, he would have too. What the fuck was the man's problem today?

"So is this your first time here?" Aldo asked after a silence of several seconds duration. "In Tahoe, I mean."

Caleb shrugged. "As far as I know."

Aldo's jaw tightened. "As far as you know. What the hell does that mean?"

It means one of us has a hearing disability, apparently. Caleb had to almost bite his tongue to keep the words from slipping out. "We've been over this already, haven't we? It means the same thing it meant last time you asked me about my past: I can't remember."

If possible, Aldo's jaws clenched tighter. "That's another thing I don't understand about you, Mitchell. How you could simply…forget everything that's happened to you?

Did someone hit you over the head or something? No, wait, let me guess; you can't remember that either, right?"

"Why is this so important to you?" Caleb glanced at him curiously. And how'd he go from being Caleb back to being Mitchell? No question about it, the guy must have heard Sally crying last night. Nothing else could explain the vague hostility he was radiating this morning.

"It's not important to me," Aldo insisted. "I'm just trying to figure out what reason anybody would have for lying about something like that."

Caleb stopped in his tracks and glared at the other man. "Are you calling me a liar, Nash? Why the fuck would I lie about something like that?"

"How should I know? Why the fuck would you all of a sudden forget half your life?"

"Boys, please, let's not fight." Sally squeezed Caleb's hand and looked at them both pleadingly.

"Look," Caleb said, making an effort to speak reasonably. "You've had mind-scrubs at work, haven't you? Why is this any different?"

"Exactly!" Aldo spread his arms wide. "That's all I'm saying. It's not a pleasant experience, but it sure doesn't leave me with years of my life missing."

Sally stirred restlessly. Caleb looked at her. "What? Can you shed some light on this?"

She shrugged. "Maybe. I mean, I could think of several possibilities. I just don't know if it's something we should be talking about right now."

"Oh for fuck's sake." Aldo glared at her. "Why the hell not, Sal? He doesn't seem to mind. And you can't claim doctor-patient privilege if you're sleeping with him."

"Hey, lighten up," Caleb cautioned. "She can do whatever she wants." Aldo glared. He shut his mouth, but the sound of his teeth grinding threatened to give Caleb a headache. "It's all right with me, you know," he told Sally. "Speak your mind. I'd like to know too."

"Well, there are many possible causes for why

psychogenic amnesia might occur—the main one obviously being a massive trauma of some sort, either physical or emotional. But it could also be intentionally produced by way of certain chemicals. Or it could be the result of some kind of posthypnotic suggestion. In your case, Caleb, it could even be caused by a program being run by one or more of your interfaces."

"So you're saying the most likely explanation is that I was hurt?"

"Oh, for—No! That's not what she's saying. Do you have any idea how badly you'd have to be hurt for that to occur?" Aldo demanded.

"No. I don't." Caleb glared menacingly at him. "Do you?"

Sally sighed. "I said in general that's the case. In your case, however...I don't think it's any more likely a scenario than any of the others, frankly."

"Like I said." Aldo stared pointedly at him before turning to Sally to ask, "So? Is there any way to fix him? There must be something that can be done about it, right?"

Caleb looked at him curiously. Bullshit it wasn't important to him. The question was *why* was it so important to him?

Sally shrugged, a thoughtful expression on her face. "It's possible, I suppose. There are a lot of things one might try. But that's a question for Caleb and his doctors to decide. If this state was induced intentionally, there might have been a very good reason for it."

"Such as?"

"I wouldn't care to speculate." Sally frowned. "Aldo, really, why all the questions?"

Caleb sighed. He didn't like to see them argue. He sure as hell didn't want to be the cause of it. "Let's just drop it. I don't know why we're still talking about this."

As soon as he got back to Oakland—or at the latest, after his stint with the Oakland PD finally ended—he was going to check himself in and get a full diagnostic done.

There was a heaviness weighing on his spirits that struck him as all wrong. For the first time he could remember, he was wondering how much he might have given up in order to get to where he was. What if he'd had a family, friends, loved ones, maybe even kids?

What if—somewhere in the world—someone was celebrating Christmas today and thinking about him, missing him. Someone who maybe didn't know what had become of him. Someone he couldn't even remember. It was a sobering thought.

Home. Family. That's what he'd been missing. That was the elusive *something* that Aldo and Sally shared with one another. He couldn't remember if he'd ever had such a thing. He had no idea if he could ever have one in the future.

There wasn't much he knew about himself when it came to this sort of thing, but what little he did know wasn't very comforting right now. Given that he couldn't imagine ever giving up either men or women on a permanent basis, he figured the odds were pretty good he was basically screwed on the home-and-family front. Maybe that was the trauma his lack of a memory was hiding?

"Caleb, you're shivering." Sally pressed against him and peered anxiously at his face. "Are you cold?"

"A little, yeah," he lied as he smiled and squeezed her hand. "I wouldn't mind heading back now. Is that all right?"

"Sure. Okay." Sally nodded and glanced at Aldo, who shrugged in acquiescence. They turned and retraced their steps through the glistening winterscape. Caleb could feel Aldo's dark, brooding gaze trained on him every step of the way, which only chilled him more. If the trail had been any more narrow, the drop down the mountainside any more sheer, or had the two of them been alone, he'd have been seriously worried right now. As it was, even despite the comforting weight of Sally's hand in his, despite the sun on his back and the prospect of the snug cabin waiting at journey's end, the trip back seemed longer and colder, and the ground beneath his feet felt rockier and more uncertain.

Chapter Eight

The knock on Caleb's bedroom door that night took him by surprise. He'd only been in bed a few minutes, having finally given up waiting either for Aldo to acknowledge his presence or Sally to give him any hint that she wanted to pick up where they'd left off the night before. Just as well, he supposed. Christmas night had to be at least as hard for her as Christmas Eve night.

As the day had progressed, Aldo's mood had gradually improved, or at least that's how it appeared to Caleb. Maybe the elaborate turkey dinner he'd insisted on cooking had distracted him from whatever had been bothering him, or maybe it was Sally's cheerful but seriously off-key singing that had done the trick. Whatever the reason, by the time the three of them were back in the living room—their mugs filled with more brandy-laced coffee, another fire blazing in the hearth, the dancing flames and colored lights once again painting Sally's hair with rainbow shades—Aldo had definitely mellowed. His previous annoyance with Caleb seemed forgotten. Instead he'd taken to ignoring him altogether, and Caleb, with typical perverseness, found he disliked that even more. He suppressed the urge to rile the other man up again, but only because he was still entranced by the warmth and closeness between Sally and Aldo. He wanted to spend a little more time basking in that glow.

Eventually, however, he'd had to concede defeat—at least for the evening. Unlike the night before, Aldo seemed in no hurry to vacate the living room. Caleb didn't know if Aldo was trying to protect Sally from anything that might cause her to break into tears again, as she had the night before, or if he was regretting inviting Caleb to share their holiday. Maybe he just wanted to spend a little time with his best friend, one-on-one. Perhaps three really was a crowd for him. It certainly wouldn't have been for Caleb, not if things had been different—if Aldo had been different—and he suspected it wouldn't have been for Sally either. It was Aldo's house, however, and maybe Caleb owed him a little courtesy.

So he'd made his excuses—and his escape. Claiming a tiredness he was far from feeling, he'd kissed Sally's cheek, wished them both good night, and taken himself to bed. Now one of them had followed him. Which one, he wondered as he got out of bed. He crossed the room to answer the door, doing his best to ignore that other small inner voice, the one that asked, which of them do you want it to be?

SALLY'S HEART WAS pounding so loud it almost drowned out the sound her knuckles made against Caleb's bedroom door. When he opened the door, wearing nothing but a pair of boxers, she couldn't even decipher the look on his face—although part of that might have been due to the explosion of heat and need the sight of him set off inside of her. She'd never seen him this close to naked before. He was breathtaking—that was indisputable. But was he happy to see her? Surprised? Disappointed? Confused? She had no idea.

"Sally, hey. What's going on?"

"Can I come in?" she asked, struggling to speak calmly, trying to quell the nerves in her stomach, the molten heat in her pussy, the far-too-shaky state of her knees. She grasped for her professional persona, that part of her that dealt with emotional encounters, awkward conversations, and all manner of unpleasantness on a daily basis, but the bitch was nowhere to be found.

"Sure." Caleb gave no sign he noticed her discomfort as he stepped back to let her in. "Everything all right?"

It was a good question. A really good question and, while they were on the subject, she really would have appreciated a hint from him as to what he thought about that. He was still hiding his own emotions, however, and so well she was forced to reconsider her abilities in that regard. Clearly, of the three of them, she was the lightweight when it came to subterfuge. At work she hid her less confident, less decisive side all day. She'd kept her darker desires hidden from Davis, and even from herself, for years. Still, Caleb and even Aldo had her beat. Both men were masters when it came to disguising how they really felt about anything.

She closed the door and leaned against it. "I've been thinking a lot about last night." She got the first part out all right, but then the memories kicked in again and she needed to take another deep breath before she could continue.

Caleb crossed his arms, his expression inscrutable. "What about it?"

Sally sighed. Fuck it. Might as well lay it out there. "I was wondering if you'd like to try again?"

"You mean tonight?" He looked surprised at that. He leaned in and rested his hand on the door above her head. "I would have thought tonight would be even harder for you," he said as he peered at her intently. "It's Christmas, after all."

Sally smiled. "I know. That's why. It's like…like I'd be giving myself a present." One she'd been thinking about, almost nonstop, since she woke up that morning, whenever she remembered the night before, on the couch, how he'd made her feel…

Caleb laughed. Leaning closer, he brushed a quick kiss across her lips. "I don't know about that. I think I'd be the one getting the presents."

"Only if I don't freak out again," she said before she could stop herself.

Caleb grimaced as he straightened up again. "Yeah, good point. About that, maybe we should take it a little more slowly. Not that I didn't enjoy myself last night but…"

"But you'd rather not end the night feeling frustrated," she said, finishing his sentence.

"Right." A swift smile, there and gone again, curled his lips. "And not that I don't want to be with you, but I don't want to rush you either. I'd rather wait until we're both sure you're ready for something like that."

"You're the one who pointed out you might not be around too long."

He nodded. "I know."

"Look." She took a step away from the door, erasing the slight distance between them once more. "The truth is I don't know when I'll ever be ready. And I'm not sure it's the kind of thing that will get easier with time, either. It might get harder. The anticipation, the expectations..."

"Sally." He touched her face. "I don't want to put that kind of pressure on you. No one should."

Which was exactly what he would say, and exactly why she wanted to do this—now, tonight, with him. Warmth blossomed in her chest. "I've also been thinking about something you said, that night at the hospital. You told me I was one of the few people who knew the real you. Well, in some ways, that's how I feel as well. About you. I feel like you know the real me."

His smile turned wicked. "Oh yeah? Why's that?" He crowded close as he spoke, taking hold of her upper arms and pushing her back against the door. Before she could answer, he slanted his mouth across hers and kissed her until her knees felt weak. "Because I know how you like to be kissed?" he asked as he nipped her jaw, her ear, her neck. "Because I know you like to be told what to do in bed? Because you like it when I take the reins?" He lifted his head and met her gaze. "You do, don't you?"

"Yes." Sally sighed. "But it's not just about control."

"Of course not," he agreed. "Sometimes you just need to be taken care of, isn't that so?"

"Maybe. Sometimes. I mean, that's part of it, for sure, but...there's more to it than that."

"Mmm. Tell me about it," he said as he pushed the collar of her shirt aside, lowered his head once again, and nuzzled her neck. "So much more."

Sally laughed. "That's not the 'more' I was talking about."

"Well, what is it then?" he asked, continuing his explorations.

"Well...I like you, for one thing," she answered. "It's

been great hanging out with you these last couple of days. And it's no secret I'm attracted to you."

"Really?" He lifted his head and looked at her curiously. "Even though I look like a kid? I thought that bothered you?"

Sally shook her head. "It did, but…well, look at you. I'd have to be out of my mind not to find you attractive. Besides, to tell you the truth, I kind of forget about how young you look when I'm with you. I'll admit that aspect scared me a little at first, and I'm still not sure how I'll handle it when we're home again but…I don't know. I'm hoping it will be okay. I haven't thought about it in days."

He nodded thoughtfully. "All right. Good to know."

"Also, I trust you." She shrugged. "I don't know why, but I do. And maybe it is because you do know all these things about me and…you're not shocked." She lifted her chin, her gaze a challenge. "I think you like it too."

He smiled again as he fitted his hands to her waist, under her shirt. "Maybe. Sometimes," he said, repeating her words back at her. "I think you're right."

His touch on her skin made her heart race, made her bold enough to rest her hands on his chest. His skin was warm there too, smooth and bare. "There's another reason I don't want to wait," she told him. "I don't know how often something like this comes along, but I don't want to miss out on something good just because I'm afraid to try."

He kissed her again. "So you think we could be something good? I do too. I think I felt that from the start. I don't know why either, but it's there. When I look at you, I feel something I haven't felt in a very long time."

"Plus, it's like you said at the hospital the other night. It doesn't have to be a lifetime commitment."

Caleb laughed again, sad and rueful. "It seems like I said a lot of things that night—and it seems like you remember them a lot more clearly than I do. What if I want it to be?"

She looked at him in surprise. "What? A lifetime

commitment? Do you think that's really possible? For people like us? For someone like you?"

He sighed and shook his head. "I don't know."

"I don't either. But right now I know I want this. I want you. C'mon, you're not going to make me beg, are you?"

Once more his smile turned wicked. "Only if you want me to."

THE SUDDEN INTAKE of Sally's breath gave Caleb his answer, told him exactly how she felt about that. Which was fine with him, because she'd been right about him too. Damn right, he liked this. He liked it a lot. "I think there will definitely be begging at some point," he said, just to tease her, just to leave the thought in the back of her mind where it could work its magic on her nerves. "But not just yet." He took hold of her hands and then started walking backward, tugging her toward the bed.

"Wait. The door," she said, steps faltering.

He stopped when they were just a couple of steps from the bed. "What about it?"

"I'm not sure it's locked." The tug of her hand in his told him she wanted to go back and double-check it.

His gaze flicked to the doorknob, then back to her face. "Don't worry about it."

That put a nice jolt in her heartbeat. He hid a grin as her brows drew together. "Don't you want to go see?"

"Why? Are you worried about Aldo? Think he might come in and catch us doing something we shouldn't?"

Her eyebrows rose. "What shouldn't we be doing?"

"Well, I know you're not *hoping* he'll join us. At least, that's what you said last night." Had that changed?

"It would be silly to keep hoping for something that's never going to happen, wouldn't it?"

"Very true." He sighed.

"We've been friends a long time. I think if we were going to be anything else, it would have happened already.

Besides, he likes men."

"You never know," he said with a shrug. "Maybe he's more like me than either of you knows."

"What does that mean?" She gazed at him curiously.

Good question. And a bad time to get into it. "Never mind. Getting back to the door, there's only one possibility left. You must be afraid of exactly what he'll see if he comes in, what I might make you do."

The hammering pace of her heart increased. Excitement danced in her eyes. "What are you going to make me do?"

"Well, for starters, I want your mouth on my dick. Now."

She glanced at the bed, but he shook his head. He indicated the floor with a nod and a glance and a flick of his fingers. Red spots appeared on her cheeks. Her breath stalled. She hesitated for a second, then lowered herself to her knees in front of him. It was hard to tell whose heart was pounding harder as he shoved his shorts down to free his cock.

She gasped a little as it popped out, erect, straining toward her, already leaking precum. One corner of his mouth kicked up in a rueful smile. Yeah, he was hard, all right. If she hadn't known it before, she did now. He'd been that way from about ten seconds after she'd closed his bedroom door.

He slid a hand into her hair and then pushed it back so he could see her face, loving the worshipful gaze she trained on him. His chest tightened until he almost couldn't breathe. It was still just a game, he reminded himself. He'd done nothing to earn that expression. Not yet. Oh, but he wanted to. He tightened his fist. The pressure on her hair drew a harsh groan from her lips.

"Well?" he asked when she continued to hesitate. "What are you waiting for?"

She leaned in and lapped at his crown with her tongue. He sucked in a startled breath when the ball of her tongue piercing dipped into the sensitive slit. Damn. He hadn't seen that move coming. She teased his cockhead for a long, luscious moment, flicking that little ball all around the crest. And that was all the teasing he could take.

"Suck me," he ordered. His voice was already husky with need. Her gaze swept up to his face. Her heavy-lidded eyes sparkled. Another of those mysterious female smiles curved her lips. She opened her mouth and swallowed him down, moving her tongue back and forth as she took him in, so that damn ball zigzagged back and forth across the vein on the underside of his cock, all the way down and all the way up again. The muscles of her throat squeezed him, and he almost saw stars. Meanwhile her hands weren't idle either. She tugged gently on his sac, rolling his balls together until he was wishing he'd had the forethought to sit down beforehand. Not that his legs were in any danger of actually giving out, but the tremors in his leg muscles, the sizzling, white-hot bursts of pleasure racing up his thighs sure made it feel like they were.

Caleb sucked in a deep breath. Holy fuck. If she kept this up, he'd be coming down her throat in no time. In his fantasies the past few nights, he'd done just that. Over and over again he'd pictured it. He'd imagined himself tightening his hand in her hair and fucking her mouth. Sometimes he'd watch her swallow his cum. Sometimes he'd paint her face with it, or those beautiful tits. That wasn't what he wanted right now, however. He still wasn't completely certain she wouldn't freak out on him again, and another night of frustration, of coming so, so close only to stop...he wasn't sure he could handle that.

"Hold on." He tugged on her hair. She sat back and looked up at him, her eyes wide and trusting, and all the things he wanted to say to her, all his plans for the evening went right out of his head. "On the bed," he told her. "Need you naked. Need to be inside you. Now."

His shorts were off in seconds. Sally's clothes took a little bit longer, but not much. Within minutes he was rolling her underneath him. "I'm sorry," he murmured as he feathered kisses along her jaw. Their hands were clasped on the mattress, fingers laced together. Her hands tightened in his. He could feel the tremors running through her. "I wanted to take things slow this first time. I wanted to tease you for hours, make you so crazy, make you beg for release. And we will do all that, I promise. But right now…" He broke off, shuddering as his cock slid along the cleft between her legs, brushing against her wet pussy. Even through the latex he could feel her moisture slicking his way. "Right now I have to be inside you. Is that all right?"

"Yes." The word was little more than a breathless hiss. "Omigod, yes," she said as she rocked her hips in increasingly frantic motions, trying to rub against his cock. He slanted his mouth across hers again and kissed her deeply. Little whimpers rose from her throat.

Caleb pulled back, breathing hard. He took hold of her legs, then hooked them over his elbows. He paused for a moment to trace the shape of her pussy with his finger, to slide that finger in and out, once again painting her arousal over her lips and the tips of her breasts.

"Damn, I love to look at you," he said as he ran his fingers over her pussy once again. "You're so sweet and hot for me, so wet." The scent of her was driving him crazy. He ran his fingers through her wetness again, then slid them between his lips. "Mmm. Delicious."

"Now," Sally begged. "Please, Caleb, now!"

He lined himself up with her opening and thrust inside. "You feel so good," he groaned as he clasped her thighs in his hands and bent her legs back toward her ears. He loved the feel of her pussy, the slick heat engulfing him as he thrust again. He craved this—craved her—and could not imagine ever having to give it up. But he still couldn't imagine giving up cocks either. So screwed, he thought as he withdrew and rocked inside her again, harder now, almost slamming himself inside her. He was pretty sure she would have liked that. Fuck. He was so damn screwed.

"Oh yeah, that's it." He groaned loudly, unable to keep the sounds inside, unable to tear his gaze away from the sight of her, laid out before him. With one hand she rolled a nipple between her fingers. Her other hand slipped between her legs to circle her clit, rubbing faster and faster. Her teeth were digging into the soft flesh of her bottom lip, and he almost stopped moving just to watch her play. "That's it," he repeated as he felt her start to come undone, her inner muscles milking his cock, her face strained and taut. Just a few more quick strokes and he was coming too. "God, I love that."

"Me too," she said, sighing in contentment.

There were many things about her that he loved. He loved how hot and wet she was, how open and vulnerable, how generous with herself, how giving. Most of all, he loved how being with her always made him feel better. That didn't mean he loved her, not yet; it just meant he was pretty sure he could learn to do so.

Chapter Nine

Aldo was baking cookies. Spicy black-pepper-cinnamon cookies—Davis's favorite. He rolled the dough thin, then cut them out using the maple-leaf cookie cutter Sally and Davis had brought him back from Vancouver. Then he decorated them with sanding sugar in a variety of colors, some in plain red or green in a nod to the season, some swirled with autumn shades of burgundy and gold, others frosted just at the tips in blue and white, as though they'd been touched by an ice fairy. Maple leaves weren't particularly Christmasy, he supposed, but he didn't care. He liked the way the cookies looked, liked the way the edges browned first, like real leaves would. Besides, he doubted anyone else here would even notice what shape cookies he made...not unless he used the pornographic cookie cutters he'd received one year as a gag gift. Too bad he wasn't in the mood to play around like that. Not when he was the only one in the house who wasn't getting any.

That was a big part of the reason he was baking, come to think of it—because he had nothing better to do. Or no *one* better to do. *No one at all to do, for that matter—but let's not go there.* And because baking cookies was part of what he'd always done at this time of year.

Of course, in years past he'd baked mostly because Davis, who had a hellacious sweet tooth, couldn't get enough of them. But Sally had always liked his cookies as well, and anything that made her happy, anything that made her feel like the world hadn't ended with Davis's death was a good thing. They both needed to feel like that. Besides, the weather had turned cold and it had been snowing for the better part of the afternoon, so going for another hike was out unless he wanted to end up with hypothermia. He could either bake or spend all his time curled up in front of the fire thinking gloomy thoughts. He'd done more than enough of that in the past few days.

He was happy Sally had found someone—truly, he was. Even if it was someone they knew so little about, someone who knew too little about himself. Someone whose very presence left Aldo feeling conflicted and confused. After a solid week of scrutiny and daily observation, Aldo was still no closer to solving the mystery that had been plaguing him. Their "vacation" time was almost over, and Aldo was beginning to despair of ever learning the truth. Were Kyle and Caleb the same person? Did it matter? What would it mean if they were? He was almost afraid to find out.

Aldo could still recall the grief he'd felt when he'd learned Kyle had been killed, the frustration when he could get no details, no answers, no closure. If it turned out Kyle hadn't died after all, Aldo didn't even know how he was supposed to feel about that. A lot would depend on why. If Kyle had been so badly hurt that this was the only option, the only way to save his life, that was one thing. He'd feel nothing but grateful then. But wouldn't Aldo have been told about it, if that were the case? There wouldn't be any reason for secrecy in that scenario. If this was something Kyle had chosen, on the other hand, if he'd made a conscious decision to off his former self... But no. No, damn it. Why would he do that? Had he thought at all what it would mean to make a total break with his past, to disappear forever? Had he even considered that he'd be breaking Aldo's heart all over again?

Aldo continued to roll out more cookie dough as he thought, slamming the rolling pin hard on the counter at the start of each pass. Maybe he wasn't being fair. After all, Aldo had been the one to end things, to break things off between them. They had been over for months before Kyle's death...his supposed death. Maybe Kyle had honestly believed it wouldn't matter to Aldo if he lived or died. Maybe he even had reason to feel that way.

Kyle had tried to contact Aldo in the weeks leading up to his disappearance, but Aldo had been incommunicado at that point, immersed in his own training, his own transformation. He didn't learn about those failed attempts to reach out to him until it was too late. Those missed calls and unread messages had preyed on his mind. They'd been a big part of Aldo's disillusionment with the military, and the main reason he'd decided to buy his way out. He'd given away his right to make his own decisions, the freedom to think for himself—to go where he needed to be, to do what he needed to do. He'd never make that mistake again.

"Everything okay in here?" Sally wandered into the kitchen to ask.

"Everything's fine." Aldo managed a smile. "Just making more cookies." He nodded toward the rack of cooling cookies. "Have some, if you like. What did you do with Caleb anyway?"

A faint blush colored Sally's cheeks. She picked up a cookie and then slid onto one of the stools across from Aldo. "He's taking a nap."

Aldo picked up the cookie cutter and began cutting out leaves. "A nap, huh?" Really? In the middle of the day? Well, why not. Once upon a time, he'd have done the same thing.

"What's your problem with him anyway?"

"Who said I had a problem?"

"Aldo, c'mon." She propped her chin in her hand and gazed at him, her expression concerned. "Talk to me. You've been moping all week. What is wrong?"

"I don't know what to tell you, Sal. I invited the guy up here for you, didn't I? I don't think I've been rude to him while he's been here."

"Of course you've been rude to him!"

Aldo slammed the cookie cutter on the counter. "Look, he's not Davis, all right? I can't pretend he is—not even for you. You can't expect me to feel the same or treat him the same or behave the same way around him. Not even if you marry him. Not even if he and I become good friends." His voice trailed off as the anger that had fueled his outburst burned off, leaving only sadness behind. "They're two different people, and that's just the way it is. I'm not even saying it's necessarily a bad thing. It's just not the same."

"I know he's not Davis. Don't you think I know that? And I know it's not going to be exactly the same. Nothing's ever going to be the same again. But I think he's becoming important to me. And you *know* you're important to me. I need to know the two of you can get along with one another."

"Well, I can't promise you that. It's too soon."

"Do you think I'm moving too fast?"

Aldo shook his head. "That's not a question for me to answer. You're only waiting on yourself, honey. Do you think you're moving too fast?"

"I don't know." She took a bite of her cookie and didn't answer right away. "Here's the thing. I think I was—maybe—getting close to being ready to move on, to go out and try again. But if I hadn't met Caleb, if he hadn't asked me out last week…then, no. I don't know that I would have started dating again just yet. I don't think I would, actually. And maybe that means this is a mistake. Maybe it would have been better if I'd met him later on. But that's not how it worked out. He's here now and…and I think he's special. So I think it would be a bigger mistake not to try. I think I can't just say to myself, well, I'm not ready, so I'll just wait until I am and then hope someone else comes along, because I might be waiting a really long time if I did that. Guys like Davis or Caleb—or you, for that matter—don't come along every day. I want to get to know him better, and I think that's either going to happen now or it's not going to happen at all."

"And I guess that's part of what bothers me." Aldo sighed. He pushed the tray of cookies he'd been decorating to the side and leaned his arms on the counter. "*Are* you getting to know him better? How? He doesn't even know himself!"

"I know," Sally said with a sigh. "I think that bothers him too."

"Well, it should. He could be anyone, Sal. Don't you think you should maybe consider what that would mean for you before you get any more involved?"

Sally smiled wanly. "Define 'more involved'? Because I think I'm already there. Anyway, what does it matter? So what if he has a different name or a different face than he did before? He'd still be the same person, wouldn't he? So maybe it's not that important after all."

"Isn't it?" Kyle had been attracted to women and Caleb certainly was, so maybe Sally was right. Maybe it didn't matter. But Kyle had also been too selfish to commit to any one person. If Caleb was the same, didn't Aldo owe it to Sally to keep her from getting hurt like that? "What if there's more to him than what you know? What if it turns out he has a whole other life somewhere that he's forgotten about? There could be a whole lot of things he's done that might make a big difference. If he's as serious about you as you seem to be getting about him, doesn't he owe it to both of you to find that out now?"

"I don't know. And I really don't understand what exactly you think either of us should do about it, even if that were the case."

"Hey, you said it yourself. There are ways to deal with it, things you can do to restore his memory—right?"

"I assume when you say 'you,' you're not referring to me specifically?"

"Of course I'm referring to you. You're a doctor. Who better to do this kind of thing?"

"Aldo...I work in the emergency room. I'm not a brain specialist! I'm certainly not qualified to deal with something like this! Besides, I said *maybe* there were things that *might* work."

"Yeah, so? It's still worth a try."

"I'm not altogether sure I agree with you on that. 'First, do no harm.' You never heard that before?"

"He's right," Caleb said, appearing in the kitchen doorway wearing jeans but no shirt, causing Aldo to all but swallow his tongue. He straightened and pulled the tray back in front of him and went back to frosting cookies. Davis had been built. Kyle, if Aldo's memory was at all accurate, had resembled a young god. Caleb put them both to shame. He was the most breathtaking sight Aldo had ever seen, nothing but lean, shredded muscles, and those shoulders... Aldo forced his pulse to stop racing, forced his breathing to slow, focused his attention on the task at hand. But anger and resentment continued its steady ascent. He was tired of wanting what he couldn't have. Tired of having temptation dangled in his face. Tired of always being alone. It had been too long.

"Caleb..." Sally shook her head. "You weren't supposed to hear any of that."

"Sorry." Caleb planted his hands on the counter on either side of her, leaned in and nibbled her neck. Aldo had to will his hand not to shake. "It's not like I do it on purpose. I hear what I hear. Besides, I'm glad I heard what you said. Both of you." He glanced at Aldo, but Aldo ignored him, so he turned back to Sally. "So. What can you do to restore my memory?"

"You too? If you heard what I said, then you know what I think. It's a decision for you and your doctors to make."

"No." Caleb shook his head. "You said it yourself; it might be intentional. If that's the case, they probably won't go for it. I want to make my own decision."

Aldo snorted. "Amen to that."

"What do we do?" Caleb asked Sally.

"I don't know. I'm not qualified to provide therapy—especially since I have no idea what's causing this. I suppose we could try hypnosis."

"You said something about drugs," Aldo reminded her.

She shot him an angry look. "Sure. There's been some very limited success with certain drugs. Benzodiazepines or thiopental, for example. But how many times must I say it? We still don't know the cause. If it's the result of some sort of brain damage, then it's unlikely anything will work."

"We won't know till we try, right?" Caleb said.

"Do you have any of that stuff with you?" Aldo asked.

"Stuff?" Sally glared at him again.

"The drugs you just mentioned."

Sally's jaw clenched. "Yes," she said at last. "As it happens, they're both used for treating seizures, and you know I never travel without emergency supplies."

Caleb chuckled as he bent to nuzzle her neck again. "That's my girl...scout."

Sally laughed, but it was a rueful sound. "Uh, Caleb, honey? You do know that the Girl Scouts don't actually have the whole be prepared thing as their motto."

"That's okay. Girls've still got it all over guys."

Aldo ground his teeth together. He couldn't take any more of this cutesy act. He picked up the tray of decorated cookies and headed toward the oven. "Caleb, if you're so damned hungry, you could just eat a cookie, you know, instead of trying to chew her ear off."

Out of the corner of his eye, Aldo saw Caleb straighten and reach for the plate of cookies. "Whoa, dude!" he exclaimed once he'd taken a bite. "You could have warned me. If I didn't know better, I'd think you were trying to blow my head off."

"Yeah, well, better enjoy it, 'cause that's all I'm gonna blow." The words were out before Aldo could stop them. Fuck. Had he really just said that out loud?

Sally made a strangled, choking sound. "Aldo!" she gasped. "I can't believe you said that."

Neither can I. "What?" he said, thinking fast, trying to bluff his way out of this, turn it into a joke...or something. "What's wrong with that? I said I'm *not* gonna blow him. D'you all of a sudden have a problem with me *not* hitting on your boyfriend? Or am I missing something? Maybe you wanna share?"

Sally shook her head, a bemused expression on her face, her cheeks bright red. Aldo wanted to kick himself. He was on the verge of apologizing when he caught sight of the knowing smirk on Caleb's face. *Fuck him.* Let him think what he wanted. "So how long is this thing going to take? 'Cause if I need to reschedule dinner, I'd like to know now."

"How long is what going to take?" Sally asked, looking even more perplexed.

He pointed at Caleb. "Whatever you're about to do to fix his memory."

"Now?" She stared at him in disbelief. "You think I'm doing this now? Why? What's the rush? I still think it would be better to wait until we're home."

Wait? Oh hell no. Aldo shook his head. He needed to know, damn it, right the fuck now. "I don't see the point in waiting."

"I don't want to wait either," Caleb told her. "I don't want to hurt you. If there's something in my past that might do that, I want to know now."

"But...tonight's New Year's Eve," Sally protested.

Aldo shrugged. "So what if it is? If this snow keeps up, we're not going to want to go out anywhere. Seems as good a time as any to me."

Caleb smiled. "Sounds like it to me too. That way, tomorrow we can start the new year with a whole new perspective. What could be better than that, right?"

A new year. Aldo sighed. This last one had sucked. He wondered if it was too much to hope the next one would be better.

* * * *

"This'll probably sting a little," Sally said later that evening as she prepared to give him the injection that would—hopefully—temporarily disable his neurotransmitters or relax whatever mental blocks had been set up to protect him from his past.

Caleb smiled reassuringly at her. "'S okay. You're not going to hurt me." He just hoped the opposite was also true—that, no matter what he found out about himself tonight, it wouldn't hurt her, either.

She'd insisted they wait until after dinner, and Caleb was certain she'd been hoping she could talk him out of it by now, but his mind was made up. Much as he hated to admit it, Aldo had a point. Caleb owed it to Sally to try and find out who he was and where he'd come from. He owed it to himself and to anyone he might have left behind. He couldn't believe he hadn't thought of that before, and that was a big part of the reason he didn't want to wait until he could bring the subject up with his "regular" doctors. He was still concerned his heightened emotions were the result of defective hardware in his brain. They'd probably want to fix it if that were the case, and once they did, he suspected this urgent desire to find out about his past would dissipate, along with everything else he was feeling.

Sally's hands were steady as she slid the needle into his vein, but her face was grim and she radiated disapproval. "Okay, now…just relax for a bit," she said after she withdrew the needle. "It's probably going to take a minute or so for it to take effect."

Caleb nodded and stretched out on the couch and tried to get comfortable. As he glanced through the window, he could see that the snow was tapering off. There were even a few faint stars visible in the clearing sky. It still looked cold, however. Inside there was a fire blazing in the hearth, and he could hear the sounds of dishes being washed in the kitchen, cupboards being opened and closed, footsteps on the hardwood floor, just the ordinary, homey sounds of people living their lives, all snug and happy…

He felt a hint of longing pierce his contentment, a tinge of uncertainty, an aching sense of nostalgia. This past week he'd tasted normal. He'd gotten a glimpse of what other people took for granted, things like home and family. Right now he never wanted to leave. He didn't want to lose what he'd found. He wanted it wrapped around him like a blanket, keeping him safe and warm.

Would he still feel like that tomorrow if tonight's experiment succeeded and he learned the truth about himself? Would he still feel like that next month, after whatever was malfunctioning inside his brain had been repaired? Would he ever feel this way again?

"How are you feeling?" Sally asked, appearing out of nowhere to eye him cautiously.

Caleb laughed. His voice sounded oddly muffled. "Funny you should ask." He took a moment to assess his condition. His mind felt relaxed even though his heart was racing and he was breathing way too fast. There was a dry, metallic taste in his mouth. "I'm feeling a little anxious. I think my brain is trying to counteract the drug. My body may be producing excess adrenaline to throw off the effects."

"Well, that's entirely possible." Sally's mouth thinned into a straight line. "It's why I don't like messing around with this when we don't know what we're dealing with."

Caleb's eyes narrowed. He stared at her intently, trying to follow the motion of that line. It had slid off both sides of her face at once and disappeared. Where had it gone?

"What does that mean?" Aldo asked. "Do you need to try something else?"

"What would you suggest?" Sally's voice sounded crisp and pointy. Its sharpness hurt his ears.

Caleb rolled his head to the side. Aldo was frowning unhappily, as though he didn't like the sound of that either, and Caleb couldn't remember when he'd arrived. "Dude. Don't look like that. She can't help it." Caleb waved a hand in the general direction of Aldo's face. He didn't like that frown. It was too serious. He did like that olive-colored sweater Aldo was wearing, however. It looked soft. He bet it smelled soft too. He wondered what it would taste like. "You need to be more like your sweater."

Aldo stared at him. Then he rolled his eyes. "Yeah, okay, never mind," he told Sally. "I don't know what you gave him, but I don't think he's throwing off the effects nearly as fast as he thinks he is."

Sally sighed. "No, I don't think so either, but I still don't want to risk it by dragging this out too long." She pulled her chair closer to the couch. "Okay, Caleb, why don't you tell me about your earliest memory. What's the first thing you remember?"

Caleb thought about that. It wasn't easy. His thoughts couldn't move in a straight line, like they wanted to do. Instead they had to slide around hard objects, trying to reach things on the other side.

"Caleb?" Sally prompted.

"Hmm." Caleb closed his eyes, the better to follow his elusive thoughts. "Learning how to use my eyes," he said at last. It seemed a very long time ago.

"What's he talking about?" Aldo again. "Are you talking about when you were a kid?"

Caleb shook his head. He opened his eyes and looked at Aldo. "These eyes," he said, pointing at his face. "The ones I have now."

Aldo's face went white. So did his knuckles, which were clenched on the arms of his chair. "They replaced your eyes?"

"No, not replaced. Rebuilt. Same as with my ears. They injected nanobots into my bloodstream, induced a coma so they could work without interference, then reconstructed or reinforced…a whole bunch of stuff, whatever they thought might be important, I guess. Afterward, I had to learn to use everything all over again."

"All right," Sally said. "Let's try and stay focused. Keep going, Caleb. You still feeling okay?"

Caleb shrugged. His chest felt constricted, and he was getting tired of lying still. He wanted to get up and move. Move? No. Fuck that. He wanted to get up and run for a couple of miles. "Heart's still fast."

"Is it getting too uncomfortable for you?" she asked. "Do you want to stop?"

He shook his head. "Keep going."

"Okay, well, let's see if we can't move you back in

time a little farther then. Can you remember the coma itself? Or anything before that?"

Caleb eyes drifted closed again as he thought about it, but all he saw was a spongy, oppressive blackness. All he heard was the pounding of his heart. Beyond that, "No. Nothing."

Sally sighed. "We're going to have to try some visualization then. And this is not something I have a lot of experience with." She was silent for a moment, so long that Caleb began to grow fidgety. Finally, "Okay, Caleb, I'd like you to imagine a door."

Caleb felt himself frown. "What kind of door?"

"That's up to you. It could be anything. Let your subconscious mind show it to you. All you need to know is that behind this door lies all your memories from your former life. Everything your mind remembers from the time before you...before the coma...that's where your mind has been keeping all those memories—keeping them safe for you. Now it's time for you to open the door and retrieve them. Do you see it yet?"

The blackness heaved and shuddered as Caleb looked around. The thundering of his heart increased its tempo. The beats had begun to blend together now into a rush of noise, like the rumbling of an earthquake, the roar of a waterfall. He shut it out as best he could and kept looking. Turning circles in his mind until, finally, "There." It was an old, wooden door, painted white. It gleamed with a faintly pearly light against the darkness, and it seemed a million miles away. "I see it."

"Okay. Good. Now I want you to walk toward it."

Caleb took one step but immediately jerked to a stop, his nerves shrieking in protest. The noise was back, even more menacing than before. Like the rattling of a freight train, the whiz of cars passing by. It was as if a locked part of his mind had suddenly opened up. A little of the darkness receded, and the source of the noise appeared right in front of him. A busy highway, crowded with vehicles all flying past him at breakneck speed, lane after lane, in both directions. There was no signal, no crosswalk, no break in the endless traffic. The door waited on the opposite side. It beckoned him. But even if he braved the traffic to reach it, even if he somehow survived, he'd still be out of luck. The door sat flush with the curb. To open the door, to get to what lay beyond it, he'd have to stop in the flow of traffic. He'd have to stand there, pull the door open. If he tried that—hell, if he even tried to cross the street at all, for that matter—he would die.

He could imagine the screeching of brakes, the blaring of horns, the cacophony of sound that would precede the impact. No, the multiple impacts from cars and trucks repeatedly slamming his body. Over and over again. *Boom. Boom. Boom.* He could imagine it too well. His muscles seized. His body jerked in sympathetic reaction. *No!*

"Sal?" Aldo's voice sounded tense, alarmed. "What's happening?"

"Supraventricular tachycardia. His heart's beating too fast. I have to give him something to slow it down."

Terror had taken control of Caleb's mind and left him trembling in fear. *Boom. Boom. Boom.* The likelihood of its own imminent destruction was the only thought his mind seemed capable of grasping. He saw himself tossed about, bouncing from vehicle to vehicle. Torn. Bleeding. Broken. It was doubtful he could survive that much damage. It was unlikely his system could override that much pain. He gasped for breath, but his chest was too tight, his lungs refused to inflate. His body flailed, and he would have fallen off the couch if Aldo wasn't suddenly there to stop him.

"Stay with me, Kyle. Come on, focus," he said as he sank to the floor by Caleb's side. He slid a hand under Caleb's shirt. His fingers felt warm and soothing as he massaged Caleb's chest. "Open your eyes, sweetheart. Look at me. C'mon, right here. Focus. I need you to breathe."

Caleb's eyes fluttered open. His gaze met Aldo's, but breathing was still not possible. He shook his head. *Can't,* he mouthed. *Can't breathe.*

"With me then." Aldo grabbed one of Caleb's hands and held it against his own chest, pressed it there. "Feel my heartbeat. Feel my lungs expand. I know you can do it. Focus. Slow your heart to match mine. Breathe with me. C'mon, baby, please."

Caleb tried. Pain knifed through his chest as he gasped for breath. His fingers clenched in the soft material of Aldo's sweater. It was just as soft as he'd been imagining, just as soft as he'd wanted it to be. But the thought this might be his only chance to feel it; his only chance to hear this soft tone, soft words, soft voice, was too much to bear. His body convulsed. His fingers tightened.

"Stay with me!"

Caleb closed his eyes. The rigor in his chest was easing. The pounding of his heart was slowing. But every breath brought fresh pain, fresh despair, an aching sense of loss rising out of nowhere.

"Kyle! No!" Aldo shoved harder at Caleb's chest, shaking him. His hand crushed Caleb's fingers.

Caleb sank deeper into the blackness. The traffic had slowed. The doorway waited. He steeled himself, took one last stuttering breath, and ran, dashing across the street to fumble with the doorknob.

The door opened in, not out; push, not pull. Caleb fell through it and found himself in another world. Behind him, the traffic dissipated, the noise receded. The highway disappeared, and then the door itself was gone...

All that was left was the lonely sound of wind blowing. Grass grew up between the bricks that lined the path beneath his feet. A narrow, uneven path built for one, it stretched away into the mist. He could follow it all the way back to the beginning, or turn around and let it carry him into the present. It was an unbroken line now, but every moment, past and future, led either here or away from this place where he now stood, this single moment in time. It was the moment that had changed everything. All his mistakes, all his regrets, each tear, each moment of unhappiness—and even his moments of love and of joy—they'd all brought him here, to this point, to this decision, to an impulse that was worthy of Aldo himself. Aldo...

Chapter Ten

Caleb's eyes shot open. He glanced around frantically. "Al?"

"It's okay. I'm right here." Their gazes met, held. For an instant Caleb's vision wavered in much the same way it had when he was relearning to see, as though his brain could not reconcile the sight before him. It was almost as though he were seeing two images superimposed upon each other. Finally, after several moments, the picture resolved. There was only one Aldo now—less hair, more beard, heavier build, definitely older—but absolutely the same man he'd known before.

"You son of a bitch." Caleb yanked his hand free of the other man's and scooted as far away from him as he could get, plastering himself against the arm of the couch. "You knew. *You fucking knew!* You bastard. What the hell, man?"

"Caleb!" Sally stroked his arm. "Calm down, sweetie. Tell me what you're feeling. What's wrong? What's going on?"

"He's what's wrong," Caleb snapped, still glaring at the man before him. "If you want to know what's going on, ask him."

Aldo's eyes were guarded as they continued to hold Caleb's, but his expression remained impassive. "I don't know what you're talking about, Mitchell," he said. His tone strived for dismissive and almost made it. It started off well, and Caleb knew he probably would have been completely taken in by it, but as the last word left Aldo's lips, his eyes widened, his face blanched.

Holy shit. Caleb's eyes widened as well as recognition hit. He knew he and Aldo had just had the same realization, had just shared the same moment of silent communication. Mitchell. His middle name. His fucking middle name. And Kay…the name Aldo had called him in his fantasies—which had not been fantasies at all, apparently, but memories from another life. K, not Kay, *not* short for Caleb, short for *Kyle*. Short for Kyle Mitchell Mosier, the man he used to be. Or Kyle Mitchell Mosier-Nash, once upon a very short time.

Caleb shoved off the couch. He couldn't sit still anymore. As he paced the floor, his mind warred with itself, refusing to accept what logic insisted had to be true. Part of him desperately wanted to explain away the facts. It had to be a mistake—or some kind of dream—it had to be, but then a log crackled in the fireplace and another puzzle piece fell into place.

He knew this place—not just from this week, but from ages ago. No wonder he'd felt so comfortable here, so completely at home.

"Is this your first time in Tahoe?"

The question Aldo had asked him days ago popped suddenly into his head. Caleb stopped in his tracks, too dizzy to move, his stomach churning with acid and betrayal, his skin crawling. *What kind of question was that? He'd known. He had to have known.* Caleb scrubbed his face with his hands. He didn't know what to think. He didn't know how to feel. This couldn't be happening.

"Caleb." Sally pulled his hands away from his face. Her eyes were filled with worry and concern. "Talk to me. Please. What's going on?"

"He knew." Caleb's voice cracked; the words came out even raspier than usual. This was not the voice he remembered either. This was his new voice, the one made rough by too many weeks of intubation. "He knew, Sal. He knew who I was. He's known all along. This whole time. He's been playing us both."

"I played you?" Aldo's face was still ashen other than two spots of color blazing on his cheeks. "Well, there's something different. Am I hearing this right? Is that the story you're selling now, Kyle? 'Cause, sweetheart, I think we both know who the real player is here."

Sally's eyes widened. "Aldo?"

Aldo shook his head. "Fuck. Don't listen to a thing he says, Sal. He's full of shit."

"That's not how it's sounding."

"Damn right it's not." Caleb laughed harshly. "Sally, do you remember what you told me the first day we were here? You said the only reason you agreed to go away with him was because he told you I was coming along. Isn't that right? Well, that's exactly how he got me here too. He told me *you* were going; he said it had been planned for weeks. So right from the start he was lying to us both."

Aldo snorted. "Oh, excuse me for trying to do something nice for the two of you. You know what, Caleb? I should have left your miserable ass back in Oakland."

"Yeah? So why didn't you, then?"

"You called him Kyle," Sally said, speaking slowly, as though she was still trying to figure things out. "Not just now. Before. On the couch. When you thought he was in trouble. He's right, isn't he? You knew who he was, even before he did."

Aldo's face went blank again—like he'd been caught out and knew it. "Stop it, Sally," he said at last. "Don't go blowing things out of proportion."

"What were you two to each other?"

Once again Caleb found his gaze locking with Aldo's. Then they both looked away. If it didn't hurt so bad, he'd have found it funny, the fact that neither of them wanted to admit to their previous stupidity, their naive assumption that their love for each other was strong enough to overcome any obstacle.

"I don't understand," Sally continued, her gaze still trained on Aldo's face. "Is this why you kept insisting we come up here?"

"How many times do we have to cover the same damn ground?" Aldo asked. "I thought it would be nice for you to get away for a little while and not be alone for the holidays. I thought the two of you might want to spend some time together, and this seemed as good a place as any. Are you telling me now that's not the case?"

"Well, this has got to be a first." Caleb shook his head in disgust. "You, pushing me at some girl? Who're you trying to kid?"

Aldo smirked. "Seems to me you just proved my point. I guess maybe I didn't know who you were after all, huh? And if anyone should be angry about this, it's me. I thought you were *dead*, damn it. All these years I've thought that."

"Right. Like you'd give a shit."

"You know, on second thought, maybe I should be asking how long you've known. 'Cause I seem to recall you claiming to be a ghost."

"When did I do that?"

"That night in the parking lot."

"Bullshit. That was just a figure of speech."

"Was it? Why should I believe you?"

"Okay, listen, you two," Sally interrupted. "You're still not answering my questions. We didn't have to come here to be together, did we? We could have stayed in Oakland. We could have worked things out."

"When she says *we*, what she really means is *us*," Caleb said, the bulk of his attention still focused on Aldo. "She and I would have been fine on our own, but I'm guessing that wasn't good enough for you. Why is that?"

"Do I really have to remind you that you wouldn't even have been able to see her if you two had stayed in Oakland? Not openly. You certainly couldn't have been seen together out in public. Or didn't Captain Douglass make that clear enough for you?"

Caleb shrugged. "It wasn't such a big deal," he lied. "We could've figured out a way around that."

"Maybe. Sure, that's possible. You've had lots of practice sneaking around, haven't you, babe? But if you care about her as much as you claim to, why the fuck would you do that to her? She still has to live in the community after you're gone, you know. She doesn't need you wrecking her reputation, leaving everyone to think she's some kind of cougar, sugar mama, I don't know what."

"Caleb?" Fear sharpened Sally's voice. "What's he talking about?"

"Nothing. He's just trying to put a self-serving spin on things, making himself out to be so altruistic when all the while he's probably plotting ways to keep us apart."

"Why would I do that?" Aldo asked. "Because I want you back?"

"I don't know. Do you? Is that why you kept harping on Sally until she agreed to help restore my memory?"

Aldo snorted. "Yeah, not likely, pal. You know what? I *should* have been trying to keep you two apart. And if I'd known for certain who you were, you can be damn sure I would have. I would have done everything in my power to make sure you never got anywhere near Sally."

"Aldo!"

Caleb pulled her close. "Don't listen to him, Sally."

"You don't know him, Sally. He's only out for himself."

"I've had enough of this," Sally said. "I want to go home—right now, tonight."

"I'm with you, babe," Caleb agreed. "I sure don't want to be stuck in this cabin with him for another minute, never mind another night. Great idea. Let's go pack."

Aldo shook his head. "What am I? The sole fucking voice of reason now? We got one vehicle, people—and it's mine, I might add. It's dark, it's been snowing all day, and on top of all of that, it's New Year's fucking Eve. Do either of you hotheads know what that means? It means the roads'll be icy. It's too dangerous to drive, and if that weren't bad enough, the only other drivers you're likely to encounter out there are probably drunk off their asses. So no. We're not going anywhere tonight."

"He's right," Caleb conceded, though it burned him to have to admit it. "It's too much of a risk. Better wait until morning."

"Fine," Sally reluctantly agreed. "But I want to go first thing in the morning. And I don't want to spend any more time listening to this tonight. I want to go to bed." She gazed meaningfully at him, slipping her hand into his as she did and squeezing it tight.

It was as clear-cut an invitation as any Caleb had ever received. One he was all too happy to accept. "Sure, let's go."

"Sally." Aldo was staring at her, his expression one of pain and disbelief. "C'mon, you're kidding, right? You're taking his word over mine?"

"I don't know who you are right now, Aldo," she said. "So just leave me alone."

As they turned to leave the room, Caleb could not help taking one last look at the man who'd once meant so much to him.

"I don't fucking believe this," Aldo muttered angrily. "How did I get to be the bad guy in this scenario?"

Caleb shook his head. "Good question. Work on that, why don't you?"

* * * *

As soon as they were in the bedroom, Caleb pulled Sally into a tight hug. She nestled against him and wrapped her arms around his waist. She was shaking so hard she might have been outside in the cold...or was that him?

"What's going on, Caleb? I need to know."

Caleb winced. He so didn't want to discuss this now. He didn't know what he did want to do, but definitely not that. "Aldo and I...we knew each other, all right? I thought you said you didn't want to listen to any more about this tonight?"

"I mean us." She raised her head and stared unhappily at him. "What was that Aldo was saying about you not seeing me in public? About me still having to live here after you're gone? We never talked about it, but what *is* going to happen after your assignment ends? Is this week all there is to it?"

Caleb shrugged. An all too familiar feeling was taking shape in his gut. Guilt. He fucking hated being made to feel guilty for being what he was.

"You can tell me, you know. I'm not gonna break. I've lost a lot more than this. And I don't regret the time we've spent together either. But I do deserve the truth."

"C'mon, Sally. You always knew I was undercover, that I'm under orders to behave in a certain way. You know I'll likely be sent someplace else once this mission is over. You can't say you're surprised. Not really."

"No, not surprised. Just…"

The sudden sheen in her eyes had Caleb wondering if she wasn't about to burst into tears. Despite all her tough words, it sure wouldn't surprise him if she did. He felt like crying too, which was a hell of a thing. Goddamn Aldo for putting them both in this position, for setting them up for this heartbreak.

Sally bit her lip. "So that's it, then? You're saying Aldo's right? That this has just been…what? A fling? No big deal? I'm never going to see you again once you leave? Is this what happened with you and Aldo? Is that why he's so mad?"

"No." Caleb let her go and started to pace. "C'mon, that's… You know better than that, don't you?"

"No. I don't understand any of it. And yes, we probably should have talked about this before, but I never expected to fall this hard for you. Still, you're not the first person with a job that takes them away for long periods of time. Either you want to try and make this work, or else Aldo was right and you've both been using me."

"I thought I told you not to listen to him. It's not as bad as he's making it out to be."

"Which part?"

"All of it, damn it!" Caleb shook his head. "Look, I'm confused too, Sally. Up until ten minutes ago I had no idea who I was. I should think that would buy me a little time to get my head straight, all right? Of course I want to figure out a way that this could work. I don't want to lose you. You're the first person in a really long time that I've actually cared about."

"Since Aldo?"

"Yeah." He sighed in defeat. "Aldo." He never thought he'd love anyone the way he'd loved Aldo. And now there was Sally. And given the way this conversation seemed to be heading, he was screwed all over again. Maybe he should just give up now, accept the inevitable, and not even wait until morning. Maybe he'd skip the heart-to-hearts, ditch them both, steal Aldo's truck, and hightail it back to Oakland.

So what if it was a holiday? So what if he was in the middle of an assignment? So what if he was leaving them stranded? They'd figure something out. Besides, his brain was malfunctioning; that qualified as an emergency, didn't it? He'd find an agency doctor and get the glitch repaired. Then he wouldn't have to feel anything anymore. Not guilt. Not grief. Not loneliness. Certainly not love.

"I know you don't want to tell me, but what was he to you? Did you two meet like you and I did, while you were on another assignment? Is that part of why he's so angry, because he knows you're going to forget about me just like you did him?"

"No!" Caleb stalked back over to where she stood and wrapped his hands around her arms. "Stop that. The two things are totally different. His issues have nothing to do with us—with you and me. I'm falling in love with you. I don't want that to end, and I hate the thought that I could ever forget you. I'll do whatever I can to keep that from happening. But he and I...it's not the same thing. We knew each other years before that, back when I was still fully human."

Sally shook her head. "What are you talking about? You're human."

"Am I? Maybe mostly, sure, but...there are times when it doesn't feel that way. I'm in a body that's so changed

I barely even recognize it, so changed that Aldo didn't even know me. What does that tell you? Because trust me, if anyone *should* have been able to recognize me, it was him. Plus…that's only on the outside. I've changed inside too—mentally, emotionally. I lose so many pieces of myself from one assignment to the next. I never even realized how much until now. I never cared about it until now. Suddenly I'm looking back on it all, and all I see are months and years that are just…cold, colorless, like all the life's been sucked out of them. Suddenly I'm realizing how much I've lost, how much I'll probably keep on losing from time to time. I'm scared, Sally. I don't want to go back to that much emptiness. I don't think I could ever forget about you. I certainly don't want to forget you! But…I never thought I could forget him, either."

"Caleb…"

Caleb sighed. He could read the question in her eyes. Much as he wished she would, he knew there was no way she was ever going to just let it go. Given the way things were going, the mess they were all in now, he and Aldo probably owed her the truth. "We were married. Is that what you wanted to know? We took vows. We made promises to one another. Empty promises, as it turned out. And when that fell apart, when he got fed up with all our problems and cut me loose, that's when I signed up for the program. Because I didn't want to live without him—or without someone in my life. It was stupid, so goddamned stupid. But…maybe I didn't want to remember anymore, maybe that's why I forgot so much. Or maybe I figured if I could become somebody else, if I could change into someone new, maybe there was an outside chance I could find love again."

He gentled his grip, stroked his hands up and down her arms, and sighed again. "But I guess the joke's on me because the more things change, the more they really do stay the same. After all these years, I found you, someone who makes me feel things again, someone I'm falling for…and I still don't know if I'm any closer to being able to keep that than I ever was."

"Of course you are. If you want it—me—that can't be impossible. We have to be able to find a way to keep this alive. Aren't you the one who said we'd work something out? That you'd do whatever you had to? I really hope you meant that because I want that too. It's too soon for promises, but I want to give this a chance. I think I love you too, you know. I think we're a lot alike, you and me. I've also lost someone I loved very much. I guess maybe we both need to believe second chances are possible, because I don't want to live without that in my life either."

"Oh, Sally." Caleb chuckled softly. "Why would you ever worry about something like that? That will never be a problem for you. You're so easy to love, sweetheart. Who wouldn't love you?"

"Oh, don't kid yourself. There have been a few."

"Really? Well, I'm sure they were all worthless bastards who didn't deserve you in the first place."

"Like Aldo?"

Caleb winced. "Yeah, well, what can I say?" He looked at her curiously. "I'm not really surprised, though. I kinda thought there'd been something like that between you two."

"Not between us," Sally said sadly. "Not like that. It was always one-sided. My own fault. I always knew he was gay. It was stupid of me to fall for him."

"No, don't say that." Caleb drew her over to the bed and sat beside her. "We love who we love, can't do anything about that. But there's nothing stupid about love. Plus, you're wrong about him. He may be the world's biggest idiot, but that doesn't mean he doesn't love you. Because, sweetheart, I know he does. I can tell."

"As a friend, sure, but no more than that. And now...if he's lying to me? If you're right and he just used me to get to you? I don't even know what to think."

"Yeah, well, I guess sometimes he just doesn't think things through like he ought to. But you know what? Fuck him; he's a moron, and I don't want to talk about him anymore. If he couldn't see what he had in either one of us, it's his loss."

"Is it really that simple?"

Caleb covered her hand with his. "No, sweetheart. Of course it isn't. I think most of the time love's a big fucking mess, not simple at all. But for tonight I'm gonna try like hell to pretend it could be. Now why don't you come here, because I'm *not* a moron and I *do* want you." He tugged lightly on her hand to draw her close, twisting around to face her as he did.

A sad smile curved her lips as she lifted her free hand and feathered her fingers along his jaw. "Oh, Caleb, I want you too."

WHEN THEIR LIPS met it was in a sweet, soft kiss. There would be no games tonight, no power plays, Sally knew it instinctively. Tonight they were just two wounded souls finding comfort in each other's arms.

Caleb slid his hand to the back of her neck. Sally melted against him. When their kisses turned heated, they pulled apart, as though by mutual, silent consent, and began to remove their clothes. There was a chill in the air. Sally didn't think the house was any colder tonight than it had been, but still the air struck her naked skin in a way it hadn't before. Given the way they both dived beneath the bedcovers, she was pretty sure they were both feeling it. They came together in the middle of the bed. She loved the way his hard body felt against hers, loved the warmth of his hands on her back.

"Caleb…" She sighed as they gazed into each other's eyes.

He smiled, a soft, tender smile as he ducked his head to nuzzle her neck. "Yeah, baby?"

She paused, a small frown furrowing her brow as a trace of uneasiness chilled the warmth. "Or should I call you Kyle now?"

He didn't answer right away. He pulled back,

frowning now too, his fingers sifting through her hair, his touch almost surprisingly tender. "I don't think so," he said at last. "I'm not him anymore."

"No?" Oh, but he'd responded quick enough when Aldo called him that, hadn't he? His name on Aldo's lips was all it had taken to pull him back to life when she'd been terrified they'd killed him. "Are you sure about that?"

"Not really. But you know what? Right now I don't care. Call me whatever you like."

Sally nodded, but the feeling that she was on the brink of losing him was not so easily vanquished. She rolled to her back, pulled at his shoulders so that he followed her down. She lifted her legs, cradling him between them, as though she could anchor him that way, as though she could hold on to what they'd once had, as though she could hold on to the past. Unfortunately it seemed a lot of his past belonged to Aldo. Probably best not to dwell on that. "Well, whoever you are, I want you to make love to me. Can you do that?"

"Of course," he said as he pressed his lips to hers again. "It would be my pleasure." He didn't need a new name to do that...or an old name...or any name at all. Hell, he hadn't even needed a real identity. He could be whatever she wanted or needed him to be. At least that hadn't changed. Or had it?

As he slid a hand down between their bodies and found her clit, his touch stayed gentle, unexpectedly so, and again, almost hesitant. It was as though he was less sure who he was now, rather than more. Damn Aldo for doing this to them. She knew she shouldn't blame him. If their roles were reversed, she'd probably have done the same. If she could bring Davis back...but would she use Aldo to do it?

Besides, the light, feathery touches were doing the job, were turning her on just as much. Her pussy was quickly on fire for Caleb, aching for more. "Caleb..."

"I need you tonight," he moaned as his lips traced over her collarbone. "I need to be inside you, need to feel you wrapped around me."

"Now," she murmured in agreement. "Take me now."

"All right, hold on a sec," he said as he pulled away. "Condom."

"Well, hurry it up," she teased as he levered himself up. All the warm air whooshed away as he lifted his body off hers and stretched out an arm to reach for the nightstand. His chest was level with her face, the small coppery nub of his nipple just inches from her mouth. So she did what anyone would do.

"Ouch!" He jerked back, his gaze surprised, as he glanced down at her. "Did you just bite me?"

She smiled back at him, showing her teeth. "Maybe."

"Oh, you're going to pay for that." He rolled to his back and quickly sheathed himself.

"I don't think so," she said as she pinned his shoulders and climbed on top. His gaze met hers again, watchful, questioning. "I think it's my turn to take the reins tonight," she told him as she reached behind her, found his cock, and lined them up. "What do you think?"

"Oh, Sal," he groaned, and unless she was mistaken, he sounded relieved. "I think that's just what I need tonight." *Because sometimes, sometimes you just need to be taken care of.*

She lowered herself onto him slowly, so slowly it dragged needy groans from both their throats. "That feels so good," she said when he was finally seated deep inside her.

"*You* feel good," he corrected her. "So tight and hot. You feel like heaven."

"I thought it was hell that was supposed to feel hot?" she teased, even as a chill raced over her skin, making her shiver. Her nipples peaked in the cool air. "Brr. It's cold up here."

"Maybe next time you'll think twice about where you sink those teeth," he told her, using his fingers to lightly brush the tips of her hard nipples.

She threw back her head and arched closer, wishing for a stronger touch there, a pinch, a sharp tug, a hint of pain—anything to blot out the cold. Instead he covered her breasts with his palms, his grip just firm enough, just possessive enough to focus her attention in a whole different way. "Caleb... God, Caleb..." She writhed in his grasp.

"Move," he murmured. His tone was closer to a plea than an order; she shivered in response all the same. "C'mon, you'll feel warmer once you start moving."

She lowered her head to gaze at him from beneath half-closed eyelids. His muscles were taut; his face was strained. She lifted herself and dropped down again, loving the way his body shook, the way his fingers dug into her flesh.

"Faster," he groaned. "Please. You're killing me here."

Power and need swirled through her. Planting her hands on his chest, she began to move, slowly raising and lowering herself.

"Damn, you feel good. You're so hot, baby, so wet." He moved his hands to her hips, guiding her, supporting her. "I love how it feels when you take me inside you, take me deep inside."

Her breathing quickened. Her pace quickened as well. She felt a flush rise in her face, and everything grew tight: the muscles of her pussy, her knees around his waist, his fingers on her hips, her fingers on his chest. "Not gonna...not gonna last," she panted. "Gotta come."

"That's right, baby," he said as he rocked his hips, taking over as her rhythm began to unravel, pounding into her. "Come for me; let me feel it. Let me see you."

She shut her eyes and gave herself over to the sensations—gave herself over to him. Then all at once, the tension broke.

His movements slowed. She slid her hands up his chest and lowered herself on top of him, still pulsing all around him. He rolled quickly, trapping her beneath him. A couple of quick, hard thrusts and he was coming too. Leaving her wishing he was bare inside her, wanting to feel the silky, warm fluid coat her insides.

"Mmm. That's better," she whispered after he'd pulled reluctantly out of her and turned away to dispose of the condom.

He paused and glanced back at her, frowning uncertainly. "What's better?" he asked as he pulled her gently back into his arms.

She frowned too. "Silly question. Everything. I feel so much better now, don't you?"

"Mmm. Much better." A relieved-looking smile curved his lips as he pulled the covers snug around them. "Very much better."

"Well, all right then. I was worried that finding out about your past might change things for us. I'm glad it's not going to."

"Me too," he agreed, but there it was again. That tiny hint of uncertainty. Sally shook her head. She should pursue it, she supposed, but she was too sleepy, too comfortable. She'd worry about it in the morning.

"Good night," she murmured, snuggling deeper into the bedding.

"Good night. Sweet dreams."

* * * *

As darkness settled around them, Caleb tried to let the steady beat of Sally's heart, the sough of her breath lull him into sleep as well. His mind was too restless, however, and his heart…his heart would not let him ignore the fact that they were not alone in the quiet house. Aldo was here too—awake in the darkness, just like Caleb.

No matter how hard he tried to put that thought from his mind, it kept intruding. Maybe it was because his memories of being Kyle were still too new. All he could think about, even now, even with Sally asleep in the circle of his arms, was how deeply in love he'd once been with Aldo. Once? He bit back a laugh. Now that they'd been awakened, those feelings were still as strong, still as raw and painful as they'd ever been. He hadn't lied to Sally. Losing Aldo had very nearly killed Kyle. For a long time he'd wished it had.

He'd screwed up in the past—he knew that. He didn't want to make that same mistake a second time. But how was he supposed to cope with being this much in love with two people—especially when those two people were friends, and when neither of them seemed overly fond of sharing? How was he supposed to cope when the morning came and they all had to face reality?

What happened when they both realized he had nothing to offer either of them beyond the present? When they both turned their backs on him and he was left with nothing but a future that would likely be as gray and featureless as his past?

It was almost enough to make him want to run screaming into the night—and maybe that wasn't even so bad an answer. Hadn't Aldo joked about all this wilderness being the perfect place to hide a body? Maybe it could hide his. Maybe he could trudge through the snow, through the crisp, stark beauty of the night until his circuits froze and his body gave out, let the soft, white snow cradle him while he drifted off to sleep. The soft, white bedding sure as hell wasn't ever going to do the trick.

Sighing in resignation, Caleb carefully slid his arm out from beneath Sally. He waited until her grumbling had subsided and she'd slipped back into a deep sleep before he slid out of bed. Then he froze again. Without his body to block it, the pale moonlight falling into the room through a gap in the shutters found her face. Miraculously it didn't wake her, just left her looking even more like an angel. He wished he could say he was going to miss her, but he wasn't even sure how long that would be true.

He dressed quickly. Less than a minute later he was leaving the room, closing the door behind him as quietly as he could.

Chapter Eleven

Aldo poured himself another drink. He couldn't believe how quickly things had fallen apart tonight, couldn't accept the fact that, this time, he might have lost Sally too.

Guys? Hell yeah. He was used to losing *them*. And unless he figured out how to stop falling for every attractive and painfully *unavailable* man who crossed his path, he'd probably lose a dozen more. But he and Sally were friends, damn it. Friends for life. Best friends. She was supposed to trust *him*. She was supposed to love *him*. She was supposed to take *his* word when something like this happened—not the word of some asshole she'd only just met.

Just because they weren't lovers didn't mean Aldo didn't still love her. Hell, he loved her more than he'd loved most of the men he'd gone to bed with over the years. Loved her, trusted her, needed her in ways he probably still hadn't discovered...

He'd always figured the two of them were in it for the long haul. He figured he stood at least half a chance of not fucking up his relationship with her—and maybe part of that was *because* they weren't lovers.

He tossed back his drink and was reaching for the bottle to pour another when the stealthy sound of footsteps climbing the stairs reached his ears. They were too quiet, too careful; he knew instantly who they belonged to. He put down his glass and turned. only slightly surprised to see that his visitor had already reached the top of the stairs. The sight still hit his overworked nerves like a fist. He jerked as though startled, his whole body on alert, a firestorm of lust igniting every nerve from head to toe, turning his cock to fucking stone.

Goddamn it. That made the second time today. Couldn't the bastard have found some other clothes to go with those low-slung jeans?

"What are you doing here?" Turning away, Aldo

picked up the bottle and willed his hand not to shake as he refilled his glass. *Ha, fat chance of that!* He was already too drunk to control his reflexes to any great extent, too drunk to even control his mouth. Liquor missed the glass and splashed over the desktop. *Fucking perfect.*

"I figured you'd want to talk."

But all that made Aldo want to do was laugh. So he did. "I can't imagine why you'd think something like that..." Shit. He didn't even know what to call the guy anymore. Kyle? Caleb? Asshole? Hey, if the slur fit...

"C'mon, Al, don't be a dick. Are you telling me you don't have anything you want to say to me? Really? After all this time? Or after all the shit you put everybody through this week just to get my memory back?"

"Nope. Can't say as I do." Aldo waved his glass as he spoke, not really caring when the whiskey sloshed up the sides; plenty more where that came from. "What's the point? You've made it real damn clear you're into women now. Hell, maybe you always were. Maybe I was just deluding myself back then. Either way, I'm through fighting it. You can do whomever you please—just as long as it's not me. And for the record, restoring your memory was *not* what this week was about. Not by a long shot. If that was even on my priority list, it was waaaay down at the bottom somewhere."

"Bullshit."

"Truth. If I did it for anyone, I did it for Sally. I hope you and she are very happy together. Just remember what I told you when I first learned you were seeing her. Don't hurt her like you did me, and I'll let you live. I do want the chance to talk to her, though, and explain *my* side of the story— assuming you haven't already turned her totally against me."

Caleb shook his head. "You really think I'd do something like that?"

Caleb, not Kyle. That was good. That's who he was now. That's how Aldo would think of him. It was easier that way.

"You think I'd hurt her or turn her against you? You

think that little of me now?"

Or maybe not. The bastard just had to keep driving home the fact that they had a past together, didn't he? "I *thought* you were dead," Aldo reminded him. "That's what I *thought*, Kyle. So how the fuck do I know what you'd do now?"

"I *was* dead, asshole. Or close enough. Not that you cared."

"Take that back." Aldo slammed his glass on the nearest surface. His hands bunched into fists. "Goddamn it, you take it back right now, or I swear I'll make you wish you *were* dead. I didn't care? My husband gets blown up or shot down or who the fuck knows—no one would even tell me how he died—and you think I didn't care? Losing you just about *killed* me."

"Yeah? Why's that? 'Cause you couldn't be bothered to return any of my calls? Or respond to even a single one of all the messages I left for you? That sounds like guilt, Al. Guilt ain't grief. It was still all about you."

"I didn't get any of your fucking messages—not until after, not until it was too fucking late. Don't you think I'd have returned them if I had? And damn right I felt guilty! Is that why you sent them? Because you knew what they'd do to me? Because you knew the thought that you'd tried to reach me and I hadn't been there would shred what was left of my heart? Well, mission accomplished, asshole, so fuck you."

"What do you want from me?" Caleb closed the distance between them. The scowl on his face raised Aldo's hackles. "You're still a self-righteous prick, you know that? What d'you want to hear me say? That I'm sorry? For what? You left *me*, remember? You're the one who called it quits, who walked away. Am I supposed to apologize for being broken up when *my* husband takes it into his head to do a fucking disappearing act? When he goes off and enlists in some stupid black-ops program and leaves me with no way to reach him?"

"Yeah, 'cause I did that for shits and giggles, right? 'Cause everything was so perfect between us? 'Cause you weren't fucking everything in sight?"

"No. I wasn't. Not the way you thought. Still, even if I had been, didn't I at least deserve the chance to talk to you, to work things out?"

"How many chances was I supposed to give you? Besides, if I recall correctly, your idea of working things out was to fuck me until I forgot why I wanted to leave in the first place."

"Well, it worked, didn't it?"

"There's a word for that kind of thing, you know, and it's not called 'working things out.'"

"Yeah. It's called 'satisfied.'"

"No, it's dysfunctional."

"Oh, lighten up." Caleb sighed. He looked tired. His face was bleak and hopeless. So was his voice as he said, "I didn't know what else to do, all right? I was fucking desperate back then, and bed always seemed like the one place I could always connect with you. After you left... Shit, I had no idea how to even find you. All I knew was that the program you'd entered had something to do with altering brain waves. And I got the stupid idea that if I enlisted in a parallel program, maybe our paths would cross."

"You're joking."

"Dead serious."

"Oh, that was a great plan." Aldo rolled his eyes, anger churning in his gut. He couldn't believe what he was hearing. Kyle had let himself get carved up, worked over, rearranged, so changed his own husband hadn't known him—and all for what? "Of all the stupid, shit-for-brains ideas. And people say *I'm* impulsive. You can't seriously be blaming me for that screwup. That's bullshit. I wasn't going to be incommunicado forever, you know. Six months. Big deal. If you really cared, you'd have waited."

"It felt like years."

"No." Aldo shook his head. "No, Kyle, it didn't. You

know what felt like years? Years—that's what. Fifteen fucking years."

"I still don't know what you expect me to say about that. Sorry you broke my heart? Sorry I didn't handle our breakup as well as *you* think I should have? What do you want from me, Al? Tell me."

"You wanna know what I want?" Need flared inside him, a hungry, howling ache that threatened to wipe out whatever was left of his common sense. He shouldn't give in to it. Should *not* do it. It wasn't fair. It wasn't right. "Well, fuck you. No! You can't just come back after all these years—come back from the dead—and just waltz in here and expect me to tell you what I want."

"Why the hell not?" A frown creased Caleb's brow. "C'mon, you bastard, I came up here tonight to try and make things right with you. Why you gotta give me such a hard time? Why can't we just—"

"Because." Aldo clenched his fists tighter. He turned away and tried hard not to think of the many times he'd imagined this moment, all the fantasies over all the years. No. It was wrong. He shouldn't do it. Shouldn't do it. Shouldn't do it. *No. Fuck that.*

As far as he knew, neither of them had ever filed for divorce. If Kyle wasn't dead—that had to mean they were still married. That had to count for something, didn't it? That had to put him somewhat in the right. He spun around and then grabbed Kyle by the shoulders. He shoved him until his back connected with one of the posts that held up the ceiling. "Because *this* is what I want, "Aldo said just before he kissed him. "The same thing I always wanted, Kyle. You."

He kissed him quick, hard and demanding, before either of them could come to their senses and change their minds. And for the first several seconds, it was bliss. Kyle's mouth was hot and wet, yielding under his. Aldo's knees threatened to give way from the pleasure, from the pressure and the taste of him. Kyle moaned low in his throat as he wrapped his arms around Aldo's waist and pulled him close.

Aldo ground his erection against Kyle's, and the friction made them both moan.

This was even better than that night in the parking lot. It was better than any dream, any fantasy, any memory, definitely any job. It was right and perfect, and it was Kyle. Kyle, who was *not* dead but right here in Aldo's loft, looking better than he had any right to after all these years, and who was about to get a serious ass whipping if Aldo found any more changes hiding inside those jeans.

Desperate to find out, he slid his fingers into the waistband of Kyle's jeans. He'd undone the top button when Kyle stopped him.

"No, wait," he gasped as he tore his mouth away from Aldo's. "Stop."

"What's wrong?" Aldo asked. He sucked in a breath as one horrifying possibility occurred to him. "Fuck. You're not gonna tell me you're sick now or something, are you?"

"No, of course not. It's Sally."

"What?" Aldo straightened in a hurry, heart stuttering in alarm. Is that why she'd seemed so pale lately, so quiet? "Sally's sick? Since when?"

"No." Laughing now, Kyle took hold of Aldo's face and pulled him back in for another kiss, soft and sweet this time. "Jeez, lighten up. No one's sick." He ran his hands over Aldo's shaved head, pressed their foreheads together for a moment, then pulled away again. "I think I love her, Al." He sounded far too serious, and much as Aldo knew he should be happy about that, he just couldn't do it.

He thrust the thought away. Maybe if he drank enough, he could forget he heard that. Write it off as just another of Kyle's lies. After all, he used to say he loved Aldo too, in exactly the same kind of sincere-sounding way. And look how far that had taken them. He probably didn't mean it now either, and in the morning…maybe Aldo could figure out what all of this meant then.

"Al? Did you hear what I said?"

"Yeah. Good for you. I love her too. That's why I'm

not going to hold it against her that she's been sleeping with my husband. You, on the other hand, still have a lot to answer for."

Kyle dropped his head back against the post and groaned. "Oh shit. You don't know how good that sounds. How much I've missed that. Hell, I didn't even know how much I missed it. But I did. Every day."

"Missed what?" Aldo frowned impatiently. "Me giving you shit for sleeping with some chick? Stick around. I'm sure it won't be the last time."

"No, not that part." A wry smile curved Kyle's lips, but his eyes misted over as he continued, "I dunno, just you being...you. And also...husband? You don't know how much I've missed thinking of myself that way. Hell, I've missed just being *able* to think of myself that way. For so long I've just been...untethered."

And I don't even know what that means. "Great." Aldo wrapped his hand around the back of Kyle's neck. Then he ravaged his mouth again. "Glad to hear it. So now maybe you'll stop fighting me and get in my bed already. I need to fuck you."

"Al," Kyle moaned, but there was a note of protest still in his voice. "C'mon..."

"What? You can have a turn later if you want. I'm not opposed to that. But right now I need to pound your tight ass until neither of us can see straight."

"Stop." Kyle's voice was firmer now. "Look, it's not that I don't want that, because, baby, you know I do. I want that more than almost anything. But if there's one thing I learned from having driven you away all those years ago, it's that wanting you wasn't enough. Even loving you wasn't enough. I thought it should be, you know? I figured we'd get married and that would satisfy you and the rest wouldn't matter. I was wrong, and I can't make that same mistake again because I don't want to lose you again."

Aldo's jaw clenched. A part of him—a really big, mad-as-hell, angry part, from the feel of it—really wanted to ask Kyle why he thought *not losing* Aldo was even an option at this point. Had he said he was willing to take Kyle's cheating ass back? Had he said he wanted anything from the man other than the chance to fuck him one more time? He was pretty sure he hadn't. On the other hand he was also pretty sure he'd be lying if he said any of those things. It might be how he wanted to feel, how he wished he could feel...but wanting and wishing didn't make it so. "So what's the problem?"

"I want to give you the commitment you need, Aldo; I do. But how the hell do I do that now that there's Sally to consider? How do I love you both, commit to you both, and not lose either of you?"

That was either a damn good question or a really fucked-up answer to his own stupid question. Aldo wasn't sure which. He shook his head. His heart felt so weighted by disappointment, it was a wonder he could still stand. Why was he even surprised? "You know what, Kyle? I don't know why you're claiming to have changed so much. What's different, huh? You're married to me, and you still want to fuck every woman you meet. And you still want me to be okay with that—and I'm not! This is the same scenario as always. I'm so sick of your lies. Pick a side, man! Are you gay or not?"

"It's not that simple."

"Yeah, actually, it is."

"Maybe for you. Do you think I chose this? Do you think I get pleasure out of hurting you? Or out of screwing up every chance for happiness I get? This isn't an act, Aldo. I'm not pretending to be something I'm not, or hiding from what I am. It's not something I'm going to outgrow. I didn't expect to fall in love with Sally, and I *never* thought I'd see you again, but I did and now I *need* you to be okay with it. Please say you'll be okay with it. Please, baby. I can't lose you again and...I can't lose her either."

"Oh, so you'd just be fucking one woman this time? Sure, that's totally different."

"You love her too. You know you do. I know you want her to be happy, same as me, and I can make her happy. I think I could make you happy too, if you'd let me. But I won't be happy without the both of you."

"I don't know what to tell you." Aldo sighed. "I don't know if I *can* be okay with it. But you know what? Right now I don't give a rat's ass about any of that. Maybe tomorrow this will still seem like a mess. Or who knows, maybe I'll wake up in the morning and it will all make perfect sense. But right now...right now I just want to make love to my husband, whom I haven't seen in fifteen years. Can we please just fucking do that? Can we, Kyle?"

"Yes, baby. Of course we can." Kyle bowed his head, and Aldo couldn't tell whether he was saying yes to him now out of desire or defeat.

Aldo wrapped both hands around the back of Kyle's neck. He used his thumbs to tilt Kyle's chin up. When their gazes connected, Aldo stopped worrying about why this was happening. The love, the yearning, the ferocious need burning in the other man's eyes was enough to stop the questions. It was almost enough to stop Aldo's breath altogether. All his doubts dissolved. This time when they kissed there was no question in his mind as to whether it was what they both wanted.

Kyle tore at Aldo's clothes. He managed to get Aldo's shirt partially off before Aldo succeeded in wrestling him across the room. After he pushed Kyle onto the bed, Aldo paused to pull his shirt off; then he followed Kyle down onto the bed. Kyle reached for him again and pulled him close. Their hands were everywhere, sliding over sleek muscles, relearning everything about each other's bodies, delving beneath waistbands to fondle and squeeze. Their breath mingled as they kissed—long, openmouthed kisses, tongues dancing together. Their legs tangled with one another, cocks straining in the confines of their jeans as they ground their hips together. The pounding of Aldo's heart beat an insistent tattoo; he needed this man, needed this man, needed this man now!

After slipping free of Kyle's arms, Aldo stood and then stripped Kyle from his jeans.

"Oh yeah. Come to papa." Aldo breathed when Kyle was finally naked. Just the sight of Kyle's penis was enough to start Aldo's mouth watering, same as always. He sank to his knees on the floor between Kyle's spread legs, his earlier urgency dissolving as he drank it all in. The brownish head, the café au lait stain along the shaft, the slight curve; all these years, he'd thought this flesh was dust. All these years, he thought he'd never gaze on it again. How many times would he have sold his soul for this moment?

It killed him to think he'd had his hands on that cock just last week and he hadn't recognized it for whose it was. Details. All those many things he couldn't imagine not remembering; it was a shock to realize he'd forgotten every one. How had he forgotten them?

He leaned in and ran his tongue up the length of it slowly, so slowly, savoring the taste, the low groan that broke from Kyle's lips as Aldo's mouth closed over that fat, brown head, the faint trembling of his muscles. Kyle was his for the taking—just like always. And just like always, Aldo wanted nothing more than to draw things out, to tease Kyle until he was wrung out and boneless, willing to swear to anything Aldo asked of him. Not that he'd mean a word of it, but maybe that had never been the point?

The urge to take Kyle hard and fast, to bury himself deep within him, to feel his balls slap against Kyle's ass was still there, still as strong as it had been all night—hell, all week, for that matter, or maybe even longer. But there was no way he could rush this. After all this time, all the years apart, there was no way he could miss a single instant.

"Fuck." The word was a breathy sob ripped loose from Kyle's chest as Aldo took him deep, opening his throat to swallow every inch. "So good…"

Years. It had been years since the last time. Surely it was that bringing the tears to Aldo's eyes. It was lack of practice, maybe a hint of nostalgia—nothing more. He pulled off slowly, twirling his tongue around the head in that way Kyle loved. It wasn't a move Aldo had planned; hell, he hadn't even remembered, until the moment he did it, about the effect he could always count on it having on his lover.

"Al...Al... Oh, fuck...fuck!"

Now that he remembered, however, he did it again, loving the sound of his name on Kyle's lips, loving the desperation in his tone, the incoherence, the broken sound of each breath. Not that his own breathing was any more steady. His chest heaved. Kyle's cock, wet and gleaming from Aldo's mouth, seemed to swell a little more each time Aldo swallowed him down. His hips bucked ever more erratically, threatening to choke Aldo until he was forced to tighten his grip on Kyle's hips just to keep him still.

Kyle's breathing quickened. Aldo picked up the pace until, almost without warning, Kyle erupted in Aldo's mouth, fluid escaping past Aldo's lips as his throat spasmed. Then Aldo was swarming on top of him again, pinning Kyle beneath him with his weight, taking his mouth again in a deep, breathless kiss.

"Pants. Off," Kyle gasped, tearing his mouth away from Aldo's. It was hard to tell who was more frantic, whose hands were less steady, but finally they were both naked, rolling together in the bedding, hands clutching and groping as they fought for dominance. Not that the outcome was in any way uncertain. Another moment and Aldo would be spreading Kyle's ass and burying himself deep. Just another moment, maybe two, since he had to get himself ready first, and then... Fuck.

The fight left Aldo abruptly. "Oh, fucking hell," he groaned, rolling onto his back to stare at the ceiling. How the fuck had he forgotten?

"Al?" Kyle turned to look at him, his gaze worried. "What's wrong?"

"I'm a moron," Aldo groaned. "That's what's wrong." He shot a fierce glance at Kyle, whose eyes were already dancing with amusement. "Don't you dare fucking say it."

Kyle's lips quirked. "Oh, come on. That's not fair." He leaned down and kissed him. "Fine. I'll play nice. Just this once, though. Now why are you a moron?"

"No lube. No condom."

"Well, looks like someone's gonna have to turn in his Boy Scout badge, now won't he? What the fuck, man? That's not like you."

"I don't suppose you brought anything with you?"

"Like I told you before, I just came up here to talk. This was your idea—not that it wasn't a good one, but still."

"Yeah, well, this isn't my room. It's a fucking guest room. Why would I keep stuff like that up here?"

"How the fuck should I know? Why're you sleeping up here in the first place? Why didn't you just... Oh." Kyle's mouth tightened. "Son of a bitch. You *did* know. You were hoping to spark my memory, weren't you?"

For an instant Aldo contemplated a lie. But what was the point? "I didn't know, okay? I *hoped*." He shook his head. "No. You know what? It wasn't even a hope. I thought I was fucking crazy for even thinking it. I thought there was no possible way it could be you, but...there was your scar and, hell, so many little things. It was driving me crazy. I had to be sure. I had to know."

Kyle studied him in silence for a moment. "And now you know."

"Yeah."

"So what're you gonna do about it?"

Aldo shook his head. For a moment he tried to focus his attention on slowing his heart rate and his breathing, on quelling the need raging through him. He gave it up when he realized all he'd be doing was trading one emotion for another, trading lust for fury, and he was getting fucking tired of being angry all the time. "I don't know. I don't know anything beyond what I want to do in this instant—which is to fuck you stupid. But that's going to have to wait until we get downstairs."

Kyle frowned. "Yeah, about that. I don't know if going downstairs is such a good idea, especially considering I left Sally asleep in your bed."

"Fucking hell." Aldo ground his teeth as anger overtook him all the same. "That's just great. Just what I wanted to think about. Another fucking mess."

"Yeah." Kyle slid his hand down Aldo's stomach. "Tell me about it." He took hold of Aldo's cock and slowly stroked.

Aldo felt himself start to relax even as his heart began to pound once again. Yeah, this would work. It wasn't what he'd wanted, but getting off was better than not getting off, no matter how it was accomplished.

"So I thought you said you wanted my ass?" Kyle asked after a moment.

"I do," Aldo said, grunting a little as Kyle's thumb spread precum over the head of Aldo's dick.

"Well, was there any particular time frame you had in mind? I kind of had the impression you were pretty desperate for it."

"Don't flatter yourself," Aldo growled. "And don't fucking tease. Or is your memory so poor you don't recall the whole no-lube-or-condom conversation we just had?"

"Do we really need a condom?" Kyle asked after another moment had passed. "I get checked pretty regularly, and if you tell me you're good, I'll believe you."

The thought of going bare, of fucking Kyle the way they used to do caused Aldo's cock to throb in anticipation and left him wanting to howl with frustration. Only Kyle would think to torture him like this, the bastard. "Great. Good to know. Definitely something to look forward to, but that still doesn't solve the no-lube problem, does it?"

"Fuck the lube." Kyle tightened his grip on Aldo's cock. "We don't need that either."

"Obviously you're mistaking me for someone else," Aldo said crossly. "And whoever he was, he must have been a real asshole. I'm not gonna fuck you dry, Kyle, so just forget it."

"If you're worried about hurting me, stop it," Kyle told him. "There are a few advantages to having all this hardware, you know. I'll be fine. Besides, like I told you before, I want you to fuck me. I want it more than anything right now."

Aldo shook his head. "Next time. Right now you can just—fuck," he said, breaking off as Kyle threw a leg over Aldo's hips and straddled him. "Now what're you doing?"

"Getting what I want," Kyle replied as he slowly lowered himself onto Aldo's cock.

Aldo gasped helplessly as he felt his cockhead breach the other man's body. "Don't be stupid. Stop, goddamn it."

"No." Kyle threw back his head, groaning as he sank all the way down until his ass rested on Aldo's thighs and Aldo's cock was lodged deep inside him.

"Move," Aldo begged as his heart began hammering. The strangling heat engulfing him was almost too much. He had to consciously slow his body's responses, or he'd have come on the spot.

Kyle fell forward to plant one hand on the mattress beside Aldo's head. His other hand fisted his cock as he began to move, rising and falling faster and faster, his hand speeding over his dick, a red flush rising up his chest and neck.

He was so fucking gorgeous that Aldo couldn't keep his hands to himself. He grabbed Kyle's hips once more, pumping his own hips as he lifted Kyle up and slammed him back down, fucking harder and faster, the two of them completely out of control. Suddenly Kyle stiffened again and groaned as he started to come. Hot spunk hit Aldo's chest. That, combined with the rippling pull of Kyle's muscles, sent him over the edge.

"Oh fuck," Kyle groaned as he collapsed on top of Aldo. "Fuck, I needed that."

"Yeah," Aldo agreed as he carefully shifted onto his

side and very, very carefully rolled Kyle off him, giving his softening cock a chance to slip free of Kyle's body without incurring injury. "Yeah. Me too."

"I've missed this," Kyle said. He pressed a kiss to Aldo's forehead, then slid lower on the bed until their gazes were level. He pulled Aldo close, eyes gleaming. "I've missed this so much."

"Ditto," Aldo replied, running Kyle's words over in his head. He missed *this*; he needed *that*. Why not the one word Aldo longed to hear; why not *him?* Anger rose within Aldo once again. A totally irrational anger because, after all, what right did he have to be angry? What right did either of them have to be angry anymore? He was sticky and sweaty and sleepy and at least some parts of him were satisfied. He guessed that would have to be enough. "Me too," he agreed, keeping his arms locked tight around the other man as they both drifted closer and closer to sleep. "I've missed this too."

* * * *

The dull thud of explosions filtered into Aldo's brain, rousing him from sleep. "Fireworks," he mumbled, watching the colored embers stream through the starry sky outside his window. They meant something, he supposed. He couldn't remember what.

"Yeah. They just started," a soft voice murmured beside him. "Happy New Year."

New Year's. Right. Aldo turned his head to find the source of the voice. Kyle was sitting up in bed, reclining against the pillows. Aldo allowed himself a moment to drink in the sight. It was a miracle that Kyle was alive, a miracle that he was sitting here at Aldo's side. Beyond those simple facts, however, lay a twisted jumble of thoughts and emotions. How the fuck were they ever going to make this work?

The wistful look on Kyle's face did not inspire Aldo with a lot of confidence in that regard. The rest of the package, all that delectable man flesh, certainly inspired a lot of other things, but confidence, no. "So," he said, not bothering to sit up himself, not bothering to pull Kyle down into another long kiss the way he wanted to either. A kiss would be nice, but it could lead to either more sex—also nice—or to another argument. That would be significantly less nice and would leave Aldo feeling stupid for having started it. "Where do we go from here?"

"I don't know." Kyle looked tired. Even his amazing eyes looked worn—especially in the too-young face—and a lot less amazing now that Aldo knew the true cost of them. He felt an urgent need to reach out to Kyle, to touch him, not just to reassure himself that he was really here, but to somehow erase all the damage that had been done to him in the name of science. Yeah, Kyle had changed, all right, but they were all surface changes. They didn't touch the heart of the man...and Aldo could not decide if that was bad or good. He felt the usual brew of guilt and grief and anger churning inside. He'd failed Kyle. They'd failed each other. And they were probably going to do so again.

"I guess we still have some things to talk about," Kyle said at last.

"Things, huh?" Yeah, no shit. Things like how did either of them overcome all the missteps and misconceptions that had brought them to this place? How did they deal with the fact that Kyle hadn't actually died? Not to mention the most pressing question of them all: how were they supposed to make things work now, when they never could before? "So fine. You wanna talk, let's talk. You go first."

Kyle's jaw clenched. "Don't you think we should wait for Sally?"

Sally. Right. Aldo winced. Another mess waiting to fall to pieces. He did not want to hurt Sally or lose her or give her one more reason to give in to despair. He did not want to dangle his relationship with Kyle-slash-Caleb in her face. Nor did he want to be the one tagging along as a permanent adjunct to the Sally-and-Caleb show; been there, done that, still had the heartache to show for it. He couldn't go there again. "Fuck. This is such a god-awful mess."

"It doesn't have to be."

"Oh no? Glad to hear it. Especially since *you're* the one who always has to make it that way. You're just never satisfied, are you?" That wasn't fair; he knew it, but he was so damned pissed off, so damned frustrated. He wanted Kyle back, needed him, and hated how out of control that made him feel. Worse, on top of worrying about whether he could even get what he needed, he had to worry about whether or not he was going to hurt Sally in the process.

"Al…"

"Of course it's gonna be a goddamned mess. When has anything between us been anything less? How happy d'you think Sally's gonna be when she finds out about us. After the way you've been fucking around with her? Not very is my guess."

"I haven't been—" Kyle stopped and shook his head. "It's not like that. I told you that earlier."

"I know that's what you said but… C'mon, man. You don't even know her, all right? This is going to fuck her up worse than before. She's been so…damned fragile since Davis's death." He gazed at Kyle accusingly. "You were supposed to be a fling. You were supposed to cheer her up, get her back in the saddle, and help make things better. You weren't supposed to be…you know…*you!*"

Kyle glared at him. "Well, I didn't know you were gonna turn out to be you either. Why the hell couldn't you have left well enough alone? If you'd kept your mouth shut and gone on pretending you hadn't recognized me, none of this would have happened. I don't think Sally or I would have even thought about restoring my memory. That was your idea. You were the one who kept bringing it up. If you hadn't, we could have all gone on in blissful ignorance."

Aldo closed his eyes wearily. And he could have gone on being lonely and miserable? No thanks. "I had to know, damn it. I needed the truth."

Kyle sighed. "Well, great. I hope it was worth it.

Because the truth is I love you both. And if you try and make me choose between you...I can't."

"Of course you'd say something like that. You haven't changed at all. I've got years of history on my side; she's got a coupla minutes on your dick. I shoulda guessed you'd weigh those both the same."

"That's not it at all."

"It's like I said earlier: same shit, different decade."

"Aldo..."

"And where do you get off assuming either of us would go along with this shit. Who says you get to choose anything? Who said either one of us would want you on those terms—or, fuck that—on any terms at all?"

"I think Sally might be okay with it. To be honest I think she'd be a lot more open to the three of us being involved with each other than you ever were."

"Oh really? You two have talked about this, have you?"

"Not exactly."

"Right. Like I said, you don't know her; you just think you do. And don't be so sure you know me anymore either."

"Look, this is stupid. I don't want to argue with you, and neither of us really knows what Sally will have to say about it. Why don't we go back to sleep? We can talk about it in the morning. Hopefully we'll all be in better moods by then."

Aldo shrugged. "Fine by me." It made sense, he guessed. If they were going to screw up all their lives, they might as well do it when well rested.

"All right, well...I guess I'll be going then."

Aldo's gut started to churn once more as he watched Kyle slide out of bed. Damn it, he should've seen this coming. He should've known. "Just hold it right there," he said as Kyle bent down to retrieve his jeans from the floor. "Where do you think you're going?" He was pretty sure he already knew the answer, but he still wanted to hear it from

Kyle's lips.

Kyle straightened slowly, a cautious expression on his face. He looked like a wild animal that had just been cornered. Or like a habitual cheater, caught once again with his pants down…or off, to be precise. Oh yeah. Aldo knew that look, all right.

"Nowhere. I just…I thought I'd go back downstairs."

"You are unbelievable; you know that? Are you actually gonna crawl out of my bed and get right back into hers? So which is it, anyway? Are you ashamed of her finding out that you're with me, despite all your promises to 'talk' in the morning, or are you just too desperate to fuck her again to wait that long? Tell me, would it have made a difference if I'd've let you top?"

"Al, come on. You know that's not it."

"No? So you're not gonna fuck her—is that what you're saying?"

"No. That is, I don't think so. I'm not planning to."

"Not planning to. Well, that's good to know. I guess you're just gonna be spontaneous, huh? Just gonna wait and see what comes up, is that it?"

Kyle closed his eyes. "Please. It's late. Let's not do this."

"Yeah." Aldo nodded. "You know what? That's the first smart thing you've said all night. And you're right. It's not just late, it's too late, so let's not do this at all. Let's just forget the whole thing. Pretend tonight never happened. You go back to being Caleb—whoever he is—and I'll go back to being the same guy I've always been."

"You don't mean that."

"You don't think so?" Aldo closed his eyes and turned away. "Well, I'd love to argue with you about that but… No, scratch that. I don't care enough anymore to argue with you. Go away, Kyle. I got nuthin' left for you."

"Al…"

"No. Just stop talking and go away."

For a long, long moment nothing happened and Aldo

could feel his temper burning away, getting shorter by the second, just like a lit fuse. If Kyle…no. Fuck that. If Caleb didn't leave soon, one of two things was going to happen. Either Aldo would get up and push him down the stairs, or he'd drag him back to bed and fuck him all over again. He wasn't sure which option would leave him feeling more satisfied.

Luckily, or not, depending on your perspective, Caleb broke first and opted for door number three—which turned out to be the least satisfying option of all. Aldo listened to his footsteps descending the stairs with a sickening sense of loss. It was better this way, he told himself. It would've never worked out. And that might have been true, but he still wished it could have been otherwise…until five minutes later, when those same familiar footsteps came leaping back up the stairs.

Aldo bit back a groan and closed his eyes tighter.

"Al? C'mon, I know you're not asleep yet. Wake up."

"Forget it," Aldo growled. If he wasn't asleep, he couldn't very well wake up, now could he? He'd love to have pointed that out, but it wasn't worth it. Instead he pulled the extra pillow over his head, kept his eyes shut tight, and even turned his face away so he wouldn't be tempted to take another look. Caleb hadn't been gone long enough to dress, and Aldo sure didn't need any more temptation. "Whatever it is, I don't care. You had a change of heart? Tough luck. Sally found out what we've been up to and threw your ass out already? Good for her. Either way, you're on your own. I can't do this with you anymore. I mean it. I'm done."

Caleb sighed in exasperation. "Could you please fucking pull your head out of your own ass long enough to think about someone else for a change? This isn't about you. It's about Sally. She's gone."

Chapter Twelve

Aldo twisted around and glared at him. "What do you mean, gone?"

"She left," Caleb told him."She's not in her room. Not in the house. She packed her stuff, took your truck, apparently, and drove away."

"Why? What did you say to her?"

"Nothing. When I got downstairs, she was already gone."

"When did this happen?"

"How the hell should I know? While we were sleeping, maybe?"

"Oh shit." Aldo sat up slowly, shaking his head in disgust. He glared at Caleb. "How could you not have noticed something like that? You're the one with the bionic ears. And that is not a quiet woman. Wouldn't something like that have woken you up?"

Caleb felt his face turn red. "Yeah, you'd think. Which is why I said *maybe* that's when it happened. It could have been…you know, before." He gestured at the bed. "We weren't exactly quiet, you know, and I sure as hell wasn't paying attention to whatever else might have been happening. You had my full attention—I promise."

"Oh, well, that's just great." Aldo sighed. "So it's my fault? Sure, of course it is. Why not? And that would also answer the question, 'why did she go?' Fuck. At least she can't get far…" His face abruptly went white. "Oh hell."

Caleb's eyes narrowed. "What do you mean she can't get far?"

"Oh fuck." Aldo dropped his head in his hands. "Fuck, fuck, fuck."

"Aldo? What did you do?"

"I…shit. I didn't want you guys to leave before I had the chance to talk to you, okay? I just wanted a chance to talk to you! I didn't want her to hate me. I didn't want her to leave here hating me because I was worried about her and...and..."

"What did you do?"

Aldo looked up at him, his eyes begging for understanding. "I siphoned off the fuel."

"Oh. Well, okay..." Caleb stared at him in confusion. "That doesn't sound so bad. So she'll have to stop somewhere for fuel."

Aldo shook his head. "There's nowhere around—not close enough. That was the whole point." He got off the bed and began to dress, pulling his clothes on rapidly.

"Look, she's not stupid," Caleb said, then stopped again when he realized she'd obviously driven off without looking at the fuel gauge. Clearly her emotions had overridden her common sense. And hadn't that been true of all of them tonight? "Okay, so she'll get stuck and have to walk back, but you said it yourself, it's not far so..."

"It's not far if it's a nice day and you're out for a hike, but it's night. It's dark; it's cold; it's been snowing all day. She's obviously upset and..." He stopped again, face twisting into a pained grimace that Caleb found not at all reassuring.

"And?" he prompted impatiently.

"And...I was already worried about her mental state. That's why I didn't want her spending the holidays alone. That was the whole reason I came up with this stupid plan in the first place. She was so depressed, and I...I was afraid she might decide to...to put herself out of her misery."

"You mean kill herself?" For the first time fear clutched at Caleb's heart. He remembered his last sight of her, her face quiet in repose, pale and peaceful in the moonlight. "So...what? You think she's going to wander off track, get lost, and freeze to death on purpose?"

"It's possible. Isn't it?"

Given the pleading tone that accompanied that question, Caleb figured Aldo was hoping he'd say no. That he'd argue for Sally's sanity and common sense. And a big part of him wanted to, but given the way his own thoughts had been trending earlier that night, when he'd felt everything was hopeless, when he was sure he was on the verge of losing both the people he loved... "Yeah, damn it. It's possible."

"Right. So we have to go get her. Hopefully before anything happens."

Caleb nodded. "Okay. What're we waiting for? Let's go."

Aldo looked him over critically. "Don't you think you might want to get dressed first?"

Caleb glanced down in surprise. Apparently sanity and common sense was in even shorter supply tonight than he'd realized. "Yeah. Good thought. Why don't I go do that?"

* * * *

Caleb shivered as they stepped outside of the snug cabin into the frosty air. He wasn't sure if the temperature had really dipped that much in the last several hours or if it was fear making him feel it more keenly as his body diverted more blood away from the surface of his body. As they headed down the drive, snow squeaked underfoot, the sound echoing in the stillness. The beam from Aldo's flashlight illuminated the ground in front of them.

"What do you think she'd do?" Caleb asked. "You know her better than I do. Would she be likely to stay with the car, or would she head back to the house?"

Aldo shrugged. "This time of night, I don't think she'd stay with the car. It's not snowing. She's not that far from civilization. It's only going to get colder. I don't know if she'd head back to the house though. I mean, why? *We're* there. That's why she left in the first place."

"Well, what other option is there? Walk into town? That would make no sense."

"No, she might stop somewhere and try to call for a cab into town. Stay overnight in one of the hotels there and maybe take a bus home tomorrow—assuming she hasn't calmed down by then, that is."

"Well, that's not a bad idea. So if she's not in the car, and we haven't run across her on the way, we can assume she's gotten a ride into town."

Aldo shook his head. "You're forgetting the *other* possibility. She might have a death wish."

"You really think that's likely?"

"With depression? I'd say it's a strong possibility."

"Well, then, we'll just have to find her."

"Yeah. Assuming we can. Fuck, it's dark. This flashlight is useless. Damn trees."

Caleb smirked. Worried as he was, he couldn't help teasing. "Not a problem for me." He pointed at his eyes. "Infrared night vision."

Aldo grimaced. For just an instant he looked like he wanted to be sick. Then his face cleared. "Yeah, well, at least now you're good for something, I guess," he muttered. He stopped and swung his flashlight in a wide arc. "Still, she could be anywhere. And look how deep that snow is."

Caleb sighed. "Yep. Plenty of places to hide a body— I remember."

Aldo was looking sick again. "Fuck. This is all my fault."

Caleb grabbed his hand and squeezed. "Oh, now, I think you have to give me at least some of the credit for that. After all, I'm the one who's sleeping with you both."

"Yeah," Aldo said drily. "Good point. That is you, isn't it?"

Despite the bitterness in Aldo's voice, Caleb took comfort from the fact that the other man had not yet pulled his hand away. "You know, I bet if we shut up for a minute I could pick up the sound of her heartbeat."

"Assuming there's anything to hear at this point."

"Would you stop that?" Caleb glared at him. "C'mon, you're not the only one who's worried, you know. We need to work together on this. I need to know I can count on you."

"What do you mean, you're counting on me?" Aldo

frowned. "Since when is this about you? I care for Sally too. And I'm the one who's spent most of the past fifteen years looking out for her. Me. Not you. And not Davis, either."

So what do you want, a medal? The words were on Caleb's lips, but he bit them back. The pain in Aldo's voice was clear and obvious; he was hurting. And Caleb just didn't have it in him to make light of that. Besides, bitching at each other wouldn't help them find Sally any faster.

Aldo gripped Caleb's hand tighter. "I know I failed you. I know I didn't give you what you needed. I failed Davis too. But that stops here. I can't keep fucking up. I refuse to lose anyone else I care about. Do you hear me?"

Caleb swallowed hard. "Yeah, baby, I hear you."

They continued walking in silence with Caleb straining his ears to hear beyond all the normal night noises: trees creaking, the near-silent flight of an owl overhead, a clump of snow dropping from a branch, not to mention all the noise he and Aldo were making.

"She couldn't have traveled too much farther," Aldo complained just as Caleb thought he heard something he could not immediately categorize.

"Shh." He clutched at Aldo's arm, bringing him to a stop, still straining to hear. There it was again. It was very faint but definite, almost lost beneath the breeze and the crackling sound of ice crystals. A rhythmic clicking sound accompanied by a shuddery sort of sigh that could be teeth chattering and the short, shivery, shallow breaths typical of hypothermia. He turned his head from side to side, trying to pinpoint her location while Aldo swept the woods with his flashlight. "A little more that way," Caleb said as he nudged Aldo's arm.

"There!" Aldo said when his beam passed over something on the slope below that reflected the light back at them. "What's that?"

Caleb moved the light aside and peered through the darkness for a better look. His heart sank. "Shit." "That" was a figure lying huddled, and much too still, on the ground under a tree a couple of yards off the downhill side of the road. Sally.

Sally blinked up at them as they slithered down the slope to crouch at her side, but she said nothing, merely hugged herself tighter. Her face was so pale her lips looked blue. She was shivering so hard she probably couldn't talk to them even if she wanted to. Given the bleak, confused look in her eyes, Caleb was not at all sure she wanted to.

"Sal?" Aldo gently cupped her head in his large hand. "You okay, babe?"

She shook her head, a jerky uncoordinated motion. "L-lost m-my ph-phone. Dropped it. Fell inna snow. Can't... Need phone. Need to c-call...call...s-s-omeone."

Caleb reached for her arm. "It's all right, sweetheart. Forget the phone. Let's just get you home."

She shrugged him off. "No. Need phone. Can't walk. T-too c-cold. Feet hurt. C-can't f-f-find ph-phone. You go 'head. Imma stay here. Rest a m-m-minute."

Aldo sighed. "C'mon, Sal, you know you can't do that. It's the hypothermia that's making you confused. You know that, don't you?"

Sally shook her head. "No. It's n-not. It's not that...that th-thing you s-said. Just s-s-sleepy 's all."

"Right. Enough talk," Caleb said as he lifted Sally from the ground and hoisted her over his shoulder. "You're coming with us. Now."

* * * *

"I'll collect the extra blankets," Aldo said when they got back to the cabin. "You get her clothes off and get her into bed. Take her in there." He pointed toward the room Caleb had been staying in. "It's got the biggest bed."

Sally was still shivering when Caleb set her down on the bed. Her eyes were half-closed and she looked like she was falling asleep. "Hang in there, sweetheart," Caleb urged. "Stay with us, all right?"

"I'm so cold," Sally moaned.

168 | PG Forte

"I know," Caleb told her as he made quick work of her clothes, intent on getting her naked and under the covers as fast as possible. "We're gonna fix that for you. Just hang on."

Sally shook her head. "I shouldn't be here," she protested as Caleb started in on his own clothes. "I don't understand. Why did you bring me back here? I was leaving, but the car..." She broke off, looking puzzled. "Something was wrong with the car."

"I know," he replied as he slipped into bed beside her and pulled her close. "Don't try to think right now. You're still confused. Just c'mere and let me hold you."

She nestled into his arms, fitting herself so perfectly against him, her head on his chest, that he would have sighed from the sheer pleasure of it if she wasn't still shivering and entirely too cold, if he wasn't still so worried. She slid her hand over his chest. Splayed fingers brushing his nipple, lodging themselves against his ribs. His skin erupted in goose bumps. "Your hands are like ice," he scolded. "Where were you trying to go, anyway?"

"I saw you," she whispered, her words almost lost between the weakness of her voice and the chattering of her teeth. "Before. You and Aldo."

Caleb sighed. No surprise there. "I'm sorry if we hurt you," he told her. "We never meant to. It just happened." Story of his love life.

Right from the start he'd known he was making a mistake. He'd known sleeping with Aldo would only lead to trouble. He'd tried to resist, but how could he? Faced with Aldo's desire for him, and his own fear that once his emotional malfunction was fixed, he might never feel anything again, how could he possibly say no to the man? How could he turn down what might be the last chance he would ever have to be with his lover again—or maybe even with either of his lovers?

Please be okay with everything, baby. I need you to be okay.

ALDO BURST INTO the room with an armful of blankets and comforters that he shook out and spread over the bed, one on top of the other. Sally sighed as each soft weight settled upon her. Soft weights. Soft shocks that shook her from her stupor. Soft blows that landed one by one by one, burying her deeper. She closed her eyes and snuggled closer to Caleb. She was suddenly desperate for the steady beating of his heart, for the hard strength of his chest beneath her cheek, desperate for more of his living, breathing warmth and maybe a little distraction.

If she thought too hard about it, all those blankets felt like shovels of dirt dropping on a casket, like snow, silent and soft, falling on an open grave. She wondered if Davis felt this cold all the time now. She shivered harder at the thought and gasped out a shuddery sob. Why, oh why had she thought about that? She couldn't bear it. She could have died herself, out there in the cold tonight, and maybe that would have been better. Why hadn't they let her? Why couldn't they have left well enough alone? At least it would be over then, and she'd be at peace. She'd be with Davis—with Davis, who loved her. She wouldn't be back here, where she didn't want to be, with Aldo and Caleb, who had each other and probably didn't want her here either. She was just in the way.

Was this how Aldo had felt all these years? Why had she never thought of that before?

"Sally?" Caleb's voice sounded concerned.

"Let me go," she pleaded quietly. "Just let me go. I don't belong here."

"That's not true," Caleb protested. He raised his head and snapped, "Aldo! Fuck the blankets already; it's enough. Just get your butt in here and help me warm her up—now!" There was a note of urgency in his voice, but Sally was past the point where she could make sense of her thoughts. Caleb's arms tightened around her, which should have felt good, which should have made her feel cared for and secure, but it just felt all wrong.

"C'mon, Sally, don't talk like that, please."

"I'm right here," Aldo said as he slipped into bed behind her, heating her back, sandwiching her in warmth. He wrapped an arm around her waist and pulled her against him. She felt the tremor that ran through him. "Sally...holy shit, you're freezing." Now it was his voice that held that urgent note.

"Really?" Caleb shifted closer, his fingers tightening on her as well. She could almost feel him glaring at Aldo as he growled, "And you're only just now figuring this out?"

Aldo ignored him. He pulled the blankets higher around her. "C'mon, babe," he whispered, his lips against her shoulder, kissing softly. "You gotta stay with us. Please, Sal. Don't you know how much I need you?" He turned his head and laid a trail of kisses all the way up her neck.

Just like Davis used to do. Another sob tore through her. The scrape of a man's beard against her bare shoulder. A man's strong thigh against her thigh, his arm wrapped tight around her middle. It was all so familiar, all so wonderful. Electricity sparked and flared...and died in the instant that she remembered. "You don't need me. Not really." She was the one who had no one, who had nothing. "You have each other."

Aldo's breath gusted against her cheek like a summer breeze. "Yeah, well, so what if we do? I mean, maybe that's true. I hope it is, but...what's that got to do with you and me? You're my best friend. I'll always need you. I think we both feel that way."

"Damn right we do," Caleb agreed. "I love you too, Sal."

Sally shook her head. "No. You're just...you're just saying that to make me feel better, but I saw you." How could they say they needed her? Why? What for? If she could get Davis back right now, if she could have that, would she ever feel the need for someone else ever again? Well, maybe. Someday. But not today.

"Sal..." Aldo sighed. "Shit. I'm sorry, sweetheart. That was my fault."

"And besides, it's not what you think," Caleb said.

Aldo snorted. "Yeah. 'Cause that always works. It's not? Really?"

"No. It's not. You two... Look, I envy what you have together, all right? I'd never want to come between you or do anything to change that. If I've hurt either one of you, I'm sorry. I never meant for that to happen. And we never meant to make you feel left out, Sally. That was never part of the plan."

"Oh, we had a plan?" Aldo again. "Well, that would have been good to know."

"It's a figure of speech, damn it," Caleb growled. "And if you think you can do a better job of explaining things, go right ahead."

Aldo shrugged. "It's not that complicated, is it? We all need each other, Sal. That's all we're trying to say. Tonight was too close a call. I thought I was gonna lose you, and it scared the fucking shit out of me. I never want to go through that hell again. Not ever. Not with either of you. I need you both, and I think you both need each other too so...fuck it. Could be this was the only way this crazy shit was ever going to work out anyway."

Caleb drew in a shuddery breath. "Do you mean that?"

Aldo nodded. "I wouldn't have said it otherwise."

"And...you're in?"

"Yeah." Aldo sighed. "I'm in. I'm all in."

Sally frowned. "In what? What's going to work? What are you talking about?"

"I'm talking about us, sweetheart," Aldo replied. "All of us. Together like this. One big, happy family. Like...I dunno. Like the three musketeers."

A sharp laugh rocked Caleb's chest. "Oh, that's original. And random. Makes me think of black leather boots and plumed hats."

"Oh yeah?" Aldo raised his head. "Want me to tell you where I'm thinking of planting one of those boots right now?"

"Not particularly." Caleb's lips quirked as he added, "Want me to tell *you* what I'd like to do with one of those big feathers?"

"I still don't understand." Sally turned to look at Aldo over her shoulder. Her nipples brushed against Caleb's chest as she moved, suddenly drawing her attention to the fact that they were all naked, in bed, pressed so close together she was aware of every twitch, every breath, every damp slide of skin on skin. Another tremor hit her, but this one had nothing to do with feeling cold. She sucked in a sharp breath. This could get awkward.

"What don't you understand?" Aldo smiled with lazy warmth as his body shifted under hers.

"Well...you're still gay, aren't you?"

Aldo's smile stretched wider. "Yeah, honey, I am. But you're talking about sex. I'm talking about something bigger than that. You love with your heart, you know, and apparently my heart doesn't give a shit about gender because I love you both and...and that's really all there is to it. I'm not willing to walk away again." He looked at Caleb as he spoke, and that expression on his face, that hint of tears in his eyes caused Sally's breath to catch. "That was a mistake."

A tremor shook Caleb as his breath caught too. Sally glanced over at him and was not surprised to see that there were tears in his eyes as well. The two men gazed at each other for a long, silent moment, and then, all at once, they both moved. Aldo's hand shot out to curve around Caleb's neck and draw him close. Caleb leaned in to press his lips against Aldo's mouth. It should have been weird, sandwiched between the two men as they kissed each other passionately. She should have felt left out, excluded—either that or really, really in the way—but she didn't. Instead she felt...a part of it all, somehow. She felt cherished, loved, and...really, really warm.

"What the fuck?" Caleb pulled away, frowning. "Al, man, what's wrong? You're burning up!"

Aldo quirked an eyebrow at him. "Yeah, what's your point? That was the idea, wasn't it? Get in bed together and warm her up, right?"

"But…okay, wait. What're you saying? You're doing it on purpose? You can do that?"

"Hey, you're not the only one who's picked up a few useful skills over the last decade and a half."

"I guess not."

"I can control quite a few bodily responses."

Caleb's gaze turned curious. "Really? Well, that's kind of hot."

Aldo chuckled. "Babe, you have no idea. Stick around and maybe I'll show you what else I'm capable of."

Caleb smiled and leaned in for another kiss. "I'd like that."

Nestled between the two men, Sally closed her eyes and drifted peacefully off to sleep.

Chapter Thirteen

A low groan reverberated through the room. Sally opened her eyes in response, heart hammering as she tried to identify the sound. Daylight filtered in through the shutters, adding to her confusion. Her memories of the previous night seemed vague, just out of reach. What was she forgetting? Why had she slept so late?

Another sound caught her ear—a slow, shuddery sigh, almost a sob. It piqued her interest. She had to know what was going on. Slowly she turned her head, trying to make the motion as imperceptible as possible. The sight that met her eyes was not what she'd been expecting, but it was enough to bring her memory flooding back, enough to bring the heat flooding back, as well. Holy fuck.

Aldo lay sprawled on the bed, still naked, looking just as sexy as she'd remembered from the handful of drunken hot-tub parties they'd attended back in their college days. The sight of him back then had fueled years of fantasies. Now it made her skin burn, made her achingly aware of her own nakedness. The heavy muscles of his chest. The dark pelt of hair. The maze of veins that tracked his arms. Even the way his hand clutched at the bedcover, as though he would rip it to shreds, had her nipples tingling and heat coiling inside her.

She lay still, grateful to be unobserved, watching with half-closed eyes. Aldo's attention was focused on the man crouching between his legs. Caleb gazed back at him, and the adoring expression in his eyes was one with which Sally had become very familiar over the past few days.

What was different was the way Caleb's lips were stretched around Aldo's cock, the way his cheeks hollowed as he sucked hard. What was different was the way his tight fist stroked his own cock, so clearly turned on by what he was doing he couldn't keep from touching himself.

Her heart beat even faster. Moisture gathered between her legs. Her pussy throbbed so demandingly she had to squeeze her thighs together to get just a little relief. She squirmed restlessly, so caught up in what she was seeing that she forgot she was pretending to be asleep.

Aldo glanced in her direction, and his eyes widened. "Fuck," he muttered as a flush colored his cheeks. He grabbed for the comforter, trying to cover himself, trying to push Caleb out of the way. "Come on, man, stop."

"Calm the fuck down," Caleb snapped. "Quit acting like some uptight virgin." He turned his gaze on Sally. "Well, what do you think?"

She shrugged. "Don't stop on my account. You guys are amazing together. I'm getting turned on just watching."

"Sally…" Aldo sighed in halfhearted protest. "Shit. That's just…that's not right."

"Yeah? Why's that?" She looked at him. "Just 'cause I'm a girl, I shouldn't like watching? Why? You're both hot—I like hot. You're both guys—I like guys. You're having sex—I like sex. Where's the surprise? Besides, it's not like it's the first time we've seen each other naked, is it? Or even slept in the same bed."

"Yeah, but…not like this."

"Oh really?" Caleb eyed Sally curiously. "Do tell."

Sally smiled at him. "Hot tubs. Spring break. Parties. We were in college together, remember? We hung out. There were a lot of late nights, a lot of lost weekends. We even shared a house for a semester. And let me tell you, he wasn't quite so much of a prude back then."

"It was a summer semester," Aldo corrected, still trying to cover himself. "Two months. And I was not a prude."

"A lot can happen in two months," Caleb pointed out, slapping his hand away. Dipping his head, he ran his tongue around the crown of Aldo's cock.

Aldo clenched his teeth, but he couldn't stop the groan that rumbled in his chest. "Stop that. Nothing happened."

"Nothing happened with me, is what he means," Sally

pointed out. "He, on the other hand, had quite the busy summer that year."

Caleb smiled. "I'm sure he did. So you're okay with this, though?"

She nodded. She was more than okay. It seemed right that they should be together. She trusted them both, cared for them both, and they clearly loved each other. Abandoning the sheet that was still partially covering her, she crawled closer to the two men.

She kissed Aldo's cheek and smiled encouragingly. "Don't let me stop you," she repeated as she ran a hand over Aldo's furry chest. "C'mon. Let me watch."

Aldo closed his eyes. "I don't fucking believe this."

"That's my girl," Caleb murmured in approval. He winked at her, then went back to work, sucking Aldo's cock. Now, however, it was Sally's face his gaze kept straying to, and she was pretty sure she could read the message his eyes were sending her, promising that her turn was coming, that Caleb's mouth would soon be driving her just as crazy.

Caleb's eyes glowed even hotter when she slipped a hand between her legs and fingered her clit, but after a couple of minutes she gave up the attempt. It wasn't enough. It wasn't doing it for her right now. She wasn't content to just sit and watch. She wanted to take part in driving Aldo out of his mind.

She scooted even closer. "Holy shit, Aldo," she whispered in his ear. "Look how deep he's taking you. I think he's gonna swallow every inch."

Aldo's eyes shot open. He turned his head to stare at her, his cheeks flushed, a scandalized expression on his face. Just as she'd been hoping, however, he couldn't keep his gaze from drifting back to Caleb once again. His tongue peeked out to wet his lips. His breath quickened as he watched his shaft, shiny and slick, disappear between Caleb's lips once again.

"You like that, don't you?" she asked.

Aldo laughed weakly. "If you have to ask that…"

Caleb glanced up at them both, a gleam of amusement in his eyes. Then his gaze met hers, the message in them clear: *keep going.*

"He likes it too," she murmured, resting her chin on Aldo's shoulder. "You know how I know that? It's because of the way he can't keep from touching himself. He's as hard as you are, and his cock is starting to drip; he's getting so wet and sticky. It just makes me want to go down there and lick it all up. Have you tasted his cum yet?" she asked, then quickly corrected herself. "Duh. Of course you have. I mean, you guys must have been together for a while. But don't you love how he tastes? Don't you love it when his cock is filling your mouth, like he's doing with yours right now? Don't you love that little noise he makes when he's getting really close?"

Aldo's breath caught. Something close to a whimper slipped past his lips. Sally laughed softly.

"Yeah," she said. She stretched up to flick her tongue around the shell of Aldo's ear. "That's right. He sounds just like that too." She ran a hand over Aldo's chest again. "So tell me, is he going to be able to swallow it all when you come? Or are you gonna flood his mouth with so much he won't be able to hold it all in?"

Aldo's eyes closed again. He dropped his head back, breathing hard and fast.

"Or maybe he won't even try," Sally continued, still sliding her fingers through the dark hair on Aldo's chest. "Maybe when your balls tighten up and he feels you start to swell, he'll pull off. Maybe he'll make you shoot that hot cum all over your chest and abs and let me watch that too."

She slid her hand over his chest and down the ridged surface of his stomach as she spoke, and that was all it took. Aldo shouted and jerked and came hard. Sally watched avidly as Caleb's throat worked and he swallowed and swallowed and swallowed… She licked her lips, barely aware she was doing it.

Caleb pulled off finally. He gave the head of Aldo's cock a final swipe with his tongue. His lips were red and swollen. They stretched into a wide grin as his gaze met Sally's. "Sweetheart, that was hot!"

Sally felt her cheeks pink up at the praise. She'd thought it was pretty hot too. And fun! And she couldn't *wait* until the two of them turned the tables and did the same to her. Her pussy was on fire just thinking about it. She hoped they'd be doing that a lot in the future.

She turned her head to find Aldo staring at her, a dazed expression on his face. "What?"

Aldo shook his head. "All these years. I had no idea you were this twisted, Sal. You must have driven Davis crazy with this shit."

Sally gasped in surprise. She felt the smile disappear from her face. A sharp pain pierced her chest. *Oh God. Davis...*

Aldo's face went blank. "Oh shit."

"You asshole." Caleb's eyes flashed with fury as he straightened up and smacked Aldo on the ass. "What the fuck is wrong with you?"

"I'm sorry," Aldo murmured as he grabbed Sally and pulled her tight against him. "I'm so sorry, babe. I meant crazy in a *good* way. You know that, right? And you know Davis always thought he was the luckiest bastard alive to have you, and now I know why."

"Nice move, Romeo," Caleb growled as he moved to sit on Sally's other side. "C'mere, sweetheart," he said as he slid an arm around her waist and tugged, trying to coax her into his arms.

She shook her head. "No, it's okay. I'm okay." And she was, mostly, but the spell was broken. The heat was gone. She didn't want to kiss Caleb now, not this soon, not when she knew she would taste another man on his lips. *Another man who wasn't Davis.* That would just make it all too real, that would just hammer home the reality that Davis was gone and never coming back. "I just...I miss him so much sometimes, but I don't want to *not* talk about him either. Even when it hurts. I don't want to ever forget him."

"You won't." Aldo pulled back far enough to look her in the eye. "I loved him too, Sal, and you don't forget people once they're that deep in your heart. Nothing could *ever* make you forget him."

On her other side, she felt Caleb stiffen. A deep sigh broke from his lips. She glanced back over her shoulder at him, surprised by the somber expression on his face. "What's wrong?" she asked as she slipped her hand into his. "Caleb?"

His eyes were bleak as they met her gaze, and his words only added to her unease. "I think we need to talk."

THE SERIOUS TONE in Caleb's voice set Aldo's nerves on edge. Something was wrong. "What's up?" he asked, striving to keep his voice level. He twisted around so he was facing Caleb. Sally kept her hand in Caleb's, but she settled against Aldo as though she felt it too. Aldo wrapped an arm around her to keep her there. This was just the way it had been after Davis died. He and Sally, united by their grief, leaning against each other for comfort, for support, for love.

Caleb sighed. "Sometimes people do forget." He shook his head. "I don't know what's going to happen when I go back to work. I don't mean here in California with you," he told Aldo. "I'm talking about afterward, when this assignment is over, when I'm recalled and sent...wherever I'm sent next. Somewhere else. I don't know what's going to happen to me." He sighed and shook his head.

Aldo watched him warily. "Go on..."

Caleb's hand tightened on Sally's. "You're the first person I've cared about in a long time," he said. "I told you that last night, and I meant it. And you—" He shifted his gaze, eyes locking with Aldo's. "Even before I remembered who you were, my feelings for you were stronger than any I could ever remember having."

"Exactly," Aldo told him. "It's like I keep saying. Your heart remembered even though you didn't think it did."

Caleb sighed. "I'd like to believe that's true, but I'm not so sure. I remember all the years in between now, and what I remember most is that I felt nothing…pretty much all the time. I think I'm not supposed to feel. And I don't know why I'm feeling things now."

"I told you why," Aldo growled, fear making him edgy. "How many times you want me to say it? You remembered. On some level, even if it wasn't conscious, you remembered me. You remembered *us*."

"I hope so. I hope that's the case; I really do. I can't tell you how much I want that to be what it is, but what if it's not? What if it's a malfunction? What if whatever's responsible for suppressing my emotions has stopped working? What if they find the problem and fix it? I don't want to forget this." He waved a hand to encompass them all. "I don't mean just the memory of it, I mean the way I feel right now. I don't want to forget how much I love you both because…if I do…I might not find my way back. I might not remember there's any reason to."

Aldo's blood all but froze in his veins. His heart seized. Sally trembled and shrank back against him, staring at Caleb. "Kay…what the fuck, man? What are you saying?"

Caleb hung his head. "I'm saying I'm scared. I signed on for a ten-year contract. Five years ago, I re-upped. Another ten years. I didn't even blink, didn't even question it. And now…what if it happens again? What if I'm gone for another fifteen years? What if I…what if I never come back? I can't expect either of you to wait forever." He looked at Sally and added, "I especially can't expect you to wait. I mean, we've only known each other a few weeks…" His gaze shifted back to Aldo's face. He winced as though he felt the force of his glare—and as angry as he was, Aldo wouldn't have doubted that was the case. "I'm sorry, Al. I guess I should have told you this last night, but everything was happening so fast and…the truth is, I didn't want to miss out on this. Even if it was the only chance I was ever going to get. No, scratch that. *Especially* if it was the only chance I was ever going to get. I love you, baby. Even if this is all the time we have. I want you to know that. I love you both."

"Oh, you know what?" Aldo snarled. "I've heard enough. Fuck that shit." He reached for Caleb. He took hold of his arm and yanked him across the bed until he was practically sprawled in Aldo's lap. His arms closed tight around him. "You hear me, Kay? Fuck. That. I don't care what happened five years ago. That's in the past. If I'd known about it, I'd have put a stop to it then. Hell, if I'd known fifteen years ago what you were planning, I'd have tracked you down and whupped your ass for even thinking about doing anything so dumb. We fucked up back then— both of us did. But you're mine, asshole, and what you do affects me. That's what marriage means: you don't get to make decisions like that all on your own, and neither do I."

Caleb nodded. "I know, but…"

"No. No buts. You were alone last time—and that was mostly my fault. That's all changed now. If it comes to a fight, I will fight for you. I'll always fight for you. You're my husband, damn it; that's gotta count for something, right?"

"Me too," Sally said. "I know I don't have the same rights as Aldo does, but as your doctor I can testify as to your condition. I can report your concerns and make sure your wishes are followed. We won't let anything happen to you, Caleb. I meant what I said last night too. I want to give this a chance. I want to make this work. We're not going to let you slip away from us. I promise."

Caleb nodded, his eyes misting up. He reached for Sally and pulled her close.

Aldo wrapped his arms around both of them. "I promise too." He knew it wouldn't be easy, though. Caleb would have to trust Aldo to keep him safe—something he'd never been able to do before. He'd have to trust Sally to not give way to despair, to continue to be there for him as well. Come to think of it, they'd both have to trust her on that count.

For their parts, Aldo and Sally would have to trust that Caleb really meant what he said; that he wasn't just paying lip service to the idea of commitment. They'd have to trust that he really did love them both—enough to return to them, even if that was still several years down a very bumpy road.

And they'd have to trust each other; that might be the hardest one of all. Did Aldo really mean what he'd told them both earlier today? Was he really okay with the idea of sharing Caleb with Sally? Was she okay with sharing Caleb with him?

All he knew for certain was that he was willing to try. No, he was more than willing. It was what he wanted more than anything in the world. But wanting and wishing did not make it so. Could they actually pull it off? No time like the present to try and find out...

He lifted his head and smiled at Sally. "I think maybe it's time we showed him how we feel, don't you?"

She looked puzzled for a moment, but then her face cleared. The smile that curled her lips was so wickedly carnal he felt it in his balls. That surprised him almost more than anything else that had occurred in the last, crazy twenty-four hours. He thought he at least knew his own heart, but maybe love was even more blind than he'd realized.

He didn't have time right now to figure out what it meant. This moment wasn't about him. This was about Caleb, making him feel loved, giving him what he needed. It was about proving to him—to them all—that Aldo could handle this. Fuck, he hoped he could handle this.

Sally scooted closer to Caleb, who was still lying sprawled across Aldo's legs. Caleb's arms closed around her. He held her close, but when she brushed her lips across his, his gaze flew to Aldo's face. Their gazes locked. In that moment Aldo knew he could stop this with a word, or hell, even without words. He could stop it with a frown. He could put an end to this whole twisted game before it even got started.

But then again, wasn't it already too late for that?

"So kiss her already," Aldo said with a shrug, trying

to sound disinterested. Caleb's arms tightened on Sally. One hand slid up to grip the back of her neck and draw her close. She melted against him, whimpering deep in her throat as he kissed her, as he took her mouth in a way that was far too familiar. Aldo shifted uncomfortably. He was half aroused, half annoyed, and the confusion of emotions only grew stronger the longer the kiss continued. He watched as Caleb's hands traveled down Sally's back. Fingers splayed on her ass, he pulled her even more snugly against him. Sally's hands tangled in Caleb's hair. Just when Aldo thought he couldn't take any more, Sally broke away.

Breathing hard, she pressed soft, openmouthed kisses along Caleb's jaw and neck. Caleb's eyes fluttered open. His gaze met Aldo's once more. Maybe there was an invitation in that heavy-lidded gaze, or maybe Aldo was just reading lust and confusion there. He couldn't be sure.

Slipping free of Caleb's embrace, Sally blazed a long, slow trail down the length of Caleb's body. Her destination was clear, and rather than think too much about that, Aldo took over where she'd left off. He shifted Caleb off his legs and leaned over the man. Caleb hooked a strong arm around Aldo's neck and pulled him down. Their mouths met in a harsh kiss that pulled a helpless groan from Caleb's throat…or maybe that wasn't what was doing it either?

Aldo lifted his head and glanced down to where Sally's head bobbed up and down, down to where Caleb's thick cock disappeared into Sally's mouth.

"Holy shit, Aldo, look how deep he's taking you. I think he's gonna swallow every inch."

Sally's voice replayed in his head. Holy shit was right. He'd thought she'd been talking like that just to get him hot, or maybe to turn Caleb on as well. It hadn't really occurred to him that maybe she'd been enjoying it too.

As he watched, she pulled off. She flicked the head of Caleb's cock with the ball of her tongue piercing, then rolled it back and forth along the slit before she swallowed him down again.

"Don't you love how he tastes? Don't you love it when his cock is filling your mouth?"

Hell yeah, he did. Aldo shook his head, amazed at his own stupidity. It had just never occurred to him to wonder whether women could feel that way. Maybe because they didn't have cocks themselves. Maybe because he didn't personally understand the appeal of het sex. Right now, however, he couldn't deny that Sally appeared to be enjoying herself. She glanced up at him and smiled, her lips stretched wide by Caleb's cock, her pupils blown, cheeks flushed, her expression dazed, and he had to admit she was more than merely enjoying herself. She was as turned on giving head as he would've been. The realization stunned him.

"Babe?" There was a note of uncertainty in Caleb's voice, a hint of anguish in the eyes that gazed up at Aldo. "Are you okay with this?"

Aldo glanced down at him and grinned. "More than okay." He pressed his lips to Caleb's, all the time thinking, hell yeah, this could work. They were three friends getting off on making each other feel good. This could totally work. The fact that they were all in love with each other to varying degrees was almost incidental; it wasn't affected by this at all. Even the fact that one of them was a woman wasn't as insurmountable an obstacle as he'd once imagined. Not that he expected he and Sally would be getting it on together, just the two of them, anytime soon, but *this* he could do.

"I'll be right back," he promised. He brushed a final, brief kiss on Caleb's lips before getting off the bed. He pulled open the drawer of the bedside table, then dug around till he found what they'd need. Condoms. Lube. He got back into bed and then slid into place behind Caleb.

Caleb groaned as Aldo spread lube over his hole, stretching and playing with him; meanwhile he used his other hand to tease one of Caleb's nipples.

"Gonna make this so good for you," he whispered in Caleb's ear. "Gonna fuck you so hard, make you come right in her mouth. I think she's gonna like that, don't you?"

A tremor ran through Sally. "So good," she moaned around Caleb's shaft.

Caleb groaned again but shook his head. "No, stop."

Aldo looked at him in surprise. Even Sally looked puzzled as she slowly sat up.

"I want to be inside her when you fuck me," Caleb told Aldo. "I want to be fucking her at the same time." He looked at Sally. "Is that okay with you?"

Sally smiled and licked her lips. "You wanna make a Caleb sandwich?" she murmured playfully. "Mm. Sounds tasty."

Aldo laughed and shook his head. "Oh hell no. You did *not* just say that."

She opened her eyes wide and gazed at him with mock innocence. "Tell me you weren't thinking the same thing."

"No comment." Aldo poked Caleb's shoulder and nodded at Sally. "C'mon, what're you waiting for?"

"Slow down," Caleb said as he moved toward Sally. "What's your rush? Haven't you ever heard of foreplay?"

"How much foreplay d'you need?" Aldo asked, watching as Caleb settled Sally higher on the bed. "She just had your dick in her mouth for the past five minutes. That's not enough?"

Caleb chuckled. "I'm not talking about me, asshole," he said as he rolled Sally underneath him. "I meant for her. And no," he added between soft kisses. "That's definitely not enough."

Aldo sighed impatiently, trying to appreciate the sight of Caleb's tight ass framed by Sally's calves. Trying to resist the urge to lean in and take a bite of that firm, delectable flesh, to pull the cheeks wide and put his tongue to work rimming Caleb's tight hole. He stroked himself slowly while he imagined it, while he thought about how good it was going to feel pounding Caleb right into the mattress...or maybe not. Probably not. Almost definitely not.

By the looks of things, it was all going to be slow and

soft and gentle from here on out. And while there was nothing wrong with any of those things, it wasn't what he was in the mood for right now.

Sally had cupped Caleb's face with her hand. Now, as Aldo watched, Caleb lifted it away, laced his fingers through hers and pinned her hand to the bed next to her head. Smiling, he speared the fingers of his other hand through her short hair, pushing it back from her face and then pulling it taut.

Sally's lips parted on a soft gasp. Excitement danced in her eyes as she gazed up at Caleb, her attention totally focused on him, totally unself-conscious, as though there were no one else around.

Caleb covered her mouth with his once more, but not like before. This kiss was almost savage. It was hard, dominant, and Aldo could tell Sally loved it. It was in the white-knuckle clasp of her fingers on Caleb's hand, the helpless whimpers that purled from her mouth. It was in the way her legs tightened around his hips.

Hell, why wouldn't she love it? Aldo wouldn't have minded a piece of that himself.

Caleb broke the kiss. He bit softly at Sally's lips, her jaw, her shoulder. Sliding down a little, he let his mouth close on one rosy nipple. As Sally moved her free hand to Caleb's head, Aldo surprised himself by catching hold of her wrist. As he pinned her hand to the bed above her head, Sally gasped. Her eyes widened in surprise.

Caleb lifted his head, glanced at the two of them, and smirked. Very deliberately, he released his hold on her other hand and used both his hands to cup her breasts, squeezing them together, using lips and teeth to worry both nipples now.

Sally's chest heaved as Aldo grabbed her hand—the one Caleb had just let go. Her eyes gleamed with excitement as he stretched that arm over her head as well. She bit down hard on her bottom lip, writhing in their clutches, an expression of delirious joy etched on her face.

Aldo adjusted his grip. As excited as Sally was becoming, he was worried she'd bite right through her lip. With the thumb of his free hand, he tried to liberate her lip, but her next move surprised him. She lifted her head, lunged after his thumb, and sucked it into her mouth. Hot lances of desire shot through his groin. *Oh fuck.* He drew in a startled breath.

Caleb slipped lower, dipping his tongue into Sally's navel, spreading her legs, stroking his fingers over the folds of pink flesh that lay between them. "So wet," he murmured in reverent tones. "So wet for me. So sweet."

A wave of tremors shook Sally's body when Caleb lowered his head to kiss her there. She gasped and bucked. Aldo slid his thumb free of her mouth. Not willing to be left out entirely, he cupped her jaw with his hand and lowered his mouth to hers.

Her lips were softer than he'd been expecting. Her skin was smooth, so smooth. But other than that, Aldo was astonished to realize that a kiss was still a kiss, irrespective of gender. Remembering how she'd reacted to Caleb's touch on her breast and curious to see if he could get the same reaction, Aldo slid his hand down her neck to her chest. He took one breast in his palm and covered it. He pressed gently, squeezing just a bit, and was astonished when she gave a little cry and stiffened, her body convulsing over and over again.

Caleb uttered soothing words as he petted and stroked for what seemed like a very long time. Eventually Sally grew still. Her breath released on a happy little sigh. She looked up at him and smiled. Caleb eased away from her then. A huge grin stretched his lips as well.

Sally tugged at his hand. Startling Aldo, who'd forgotten he was still holding her. He let go of her wrists and sat back, not knowing what to expect. Next thing he knew, he was flat on his back, with Caleb swarming on top of him. Their cocks knocked and rubbed together as they wrestled. "Now *that's* enough foreplay," Caleb said, smiling smugly down at Aldo. "Just so you'll know, for next time."

Aldo hooked a leg over his and reversed their positions, flipping Caleb onto his back. "Almost enough," he corrected as he took Caleb's mouth in a punishing kiss. There was an odd taste to Caleb's lips. Aldo could only imagine it was Sally, but he pushed the thought away. It was too much to take in all at once. He raised his head and looked down at Caleb. "I need to fuck you now," he told him.

Caleb nodded. "Hell yes."

As soon as Aldo let him up, Caleb returned to Sally, who'd been watching them with a misty expression on her face. Caleb took her chin in his hand and kissed her every bit as passionately as he'd just kissed Aldo. He hugged her, and she hugged him back, but her eyes searched out Aldo's over Caleb's shoulder. When she reached a hand to him as well, Aldo took it in his and softly kissed her knuckles.

He winked at her as he dropped her hand; then he smacked Caleb on the shoulder. "C'mon, man, suit up already," he said as he handed him a condom. "I'm not getting any younger here."

As he tore open a second condom for himself, Caleb looked at him questioningly.

Aldo shrugged. Yeah, it wasn't what he wanted either. "For now," he told him. "We still have a lot to figure out."

Caleb nodded reluctantly.

Condom in place, Caleb turned back to Sally once again. She reached for him and pulled him close. "Now it's your turn," she murmured as she wrapped her legs around his waist. "We're going to make this so good for you."

Caleb lifted her hips, positioning himself at her opening, and slowly thrust inside. He fell forward onto his elbows and spread his own legs just enough so that Aldo had access.

Aldo knelt behind him. After slicking his shaft with the lube, he poured more down the crease of Caleb's ass before tossing the bottle aside. He spread Caleb's cheeks and used his thumb to rub over the tightly puckered opening, teasing and loosening, spearing and stretching. He pumped his fingers in and out of Caleb's ass, stretching his hole even as Caleb pumped slowly into Sally.

He was mesmerized by the sight and sounds of them. The flush on Sally's face, her breathy little sighs, Caleb's soft grunts of pleasure, the flex of his hips as he ground into her. Finally Aldo could wait no longer.

He put a hand on Caleb's back, lined up the head of his cock with Caleb's entrance, and at Caleb's next stroke, he pushed forward with him, just breaching him. Caleb shuddered and stilled. Aldo grabbed hold of Caleb's hips and pulled him back against him. The motion pushed Aldo's cock deeper into Caleb's ass. Caleb groaned and pushed forward into Sally, slipping partially off Aldo's cock. Aldo followed after him, pushing into him again, and then pulling them both back once more. Forward and back they went as they slowly found their rhythm together. Each time, Aldo seated himself a little deeper; each time, Caleb moved a little faster. Sally bit her lip, breathing hard as she watched them both with wide, excited eyes, groaning each time Caleb thrust into her.

Aldo dug his fingers harder into Caleb's hips as the pace intensified. The room filled with the sounds of their lovemaking, moans and whimpers and the slap of skin against skin. Caleb bent his head to nuzzle Sally's neck. Her hands clutched him tight—one at his shoulder, nails biting into the muscles there; the other cupping his skull. Aldo leaned forward and sank his teeth into Caleb's other shoulder, eliciting a long, heartfelt groan that Sally seemed to echo.

And then Sally was stiffening in Caleb's arms once again. Caleb gave a hoarse cry as well, and then he was coming, the muscles in his ass milking Aldo's cock.

Aldo clutched harder at Caleb's hips, pumped a couple more times, and then shot deep in Caleb's ass, wishing like hell he'd had the sense to ditch the condom, wanting to mark Caleb as his, inside and out.

He collapsed on Caleb's back, breathing deep, soaking in the pleasure of having him back again, only vaguely aware of something hard digging into his abdomen and far too sated to care. He was startled when Caleb bucked beneath him. "Stop that. I'm trying to enjoy the afterglow."

"And I'm trying to keep from falling over," Caleb growled, his voice strained, his arms shaking. "You weigh a damn ton. Off!" The violence in his tone shocked Aldo until he realized the hard objects poking into his stomach were Sally's legs, and that Caleb was using all his strength to keep the two of them from crushing her.

"Shit." Aldo pulled away quickly. He rolled to his left and landed on his back beside Sally. "I guess we'll need to work on those damned dismounts, huh?"

Caleb chuckled. "We?" He shared a smile with Sally as he dropped to the bed on her opposite side. "Speak for yourself."

"Ah, bite me." Aldo winked at Sally. "Sandwich fillings don't get to complain."

Sally giggled and stretched lazily. Then a small frown appeared on her forehead "Why'd you have to bring up food? Now I'm hungry."

"You're still hungry?" Aldo arched an eyebrow. He was on the verge of making a joke, to ask if Caleb's lunchmeat hadn't been enough of a mouthful for her. It was the kind of thing he'd say to Caleb, after all, but *holy fuck*, what was he thinking? He could not say something like that to Sally…could he? Well, not today, at any rate. He shook his head. "Sorry, sweetheart, but I'm afraid you're on your own with that. Scrounge up whatever you want. Me, I don't plan on leaving this bed until at least tomorrow morning." He grabbed a pillow and stuffed it under his head, then noticed the odd look on Caleb's face. "What?"

Caleb's mouth curved in a crooked smile. "Thank you."

Aldo frowned. "What for? Being too lazy to cook? Only taking one pillow? Whatever. You're welcome."

Caleb shook his head. "I'm serious, man. When you said you were okay with this, I thought…well, I guess I thought that meant you'd maybe try and look the other way, pretend it wasn't happening or something. I thought—at most—it meant you wouldn't be so fast to walk away again. I never imagined you'd get so…involved."

Involved…yeah, that was one word for it, all right. Aldo shrugged. "Yeah, well, it wasn't exactly what I ever imagined either. Live and learn, right?"

"And, you"—Caleb turned to Sally—"shit, we didn't even discuss this and here you are and…" He broke off again, obviously lost for words.

"We did kind of discuss it," Sally said, biting her lip a little as Aldo turned to stare at her.

Caleb shrugged. "Not really. Not as something…permanent."

"Wait a minute," Aldo said, staring at both of them in turn now. "You two discussed *this*? The three of us?"

"Like I said," Caleb repeated. "Not like this. More as…I dunno. A fantasy, I guess."

Aldo rolled his eyes. "Yeah, 'cause, we both know you'd never act on something like that."

Sally let out a sigh. "Oh, Aldo, stop. And don't act like you're so surprised. You always knew how I felt about you. I'm not saying I understand this any better than you do, but don't try and tell me you didn't enjoy it at least a little. It feels…right, somehow."

"I guess…" Now it was Aldo who was lost for words. He snagged one of Sally's hands and held it tight. "Whatever, babe. You know I love you. You know I'll do whatever I can to make you happy."

"And I love you too," Caleb said. "Both of you."

Aldo smiled. Here, at last, was something he knew how to respond to. "Damn right you do," he said as he met the look in his husband's eyes, a look he'd never thought to see again. "This time, don't forget it."

Chapter Fourteen

Six years later…

It was another perfect winter morning. Crisp, pine-scented air. Blue sky overhead. Fresh snow underfoot. Caleb glanced around, enjoying it all, especially the company—the man with whom he was holding hands.

"I guess it's true what they say." Aldo sighed, as he too looked around, taking in the scenery. "The more things change, the more they don't really change at all."

Caleb rolled his eyes. "Who says that?" he couldn't help asking. "C'mon, no one says that. That's not even how it goes, and anyway, it's not true. There've been a lot of changes. How can you say there haven't?" The last six years had seen plenty of changes and plenty of challenges for them all, not to mention more close calls than he cared to think about. There had even been changes of a more personal nature—like the gray hairs that had begun to appear in Aldo's beard or the fact that, now that his body was no longer being kept artificially young, Caleb was starting to look and feel closer to his actual age.

"You know what I mean," Aldo protested. "At the end of the day…here we are again. It's New Year's Day. We're back in Tahoe…"

"You're still crazy about me."

"I think you mean *you're* still crazy about *me*, don't you?"

"That too, I guess."

"Exactly." Aldo's smile turned smug. "See? Just like I said. No changes whatsoever."

"Except that nowadays you actually believe me when I say that."

Aldo shook his head. "Okay, well, if you gotta spoil the mood by bringing up ancient history, go right ahead. But you know I've believed you for a long time now. You can't say I haven't."

"I know." Caleb gave his hand a squeeze. "Now, if you're done being all philosophical, why don't you tell me why you dragged me out here in the cold this morning? Pretty as it is, we could be back in our nice, warm bed."

Aldo sighed. "Philosophical? Yeah, that's me, all right." The look on his face as he reached for Caleb's other hand was so suddenly and unexpectedly serious that, for just an instant Caleb was worried he was about to get bad news.

Caleb's eyebrows rose. "Al? What's up?"

"It's just what I've been trying to tell you. Some things don't change. Or, even if they do change, even when they change completely, at heart they're still the same. Like you and me."

Caleb nodded. "Clear as mud."

"Would you just shut up and let me talk?" Aldo snapped. "Look...I love you. Okay? I've always loved you, and at this point I think it's safe to say I always will. So...I want you to marry me. You know, again."

"Okay." Caleb frowned. "But...I mean, we're already married. So how is this supposed to work?"

Aldo rolled his eyes. "Yeah, well, fine. But 'I'd like you to renew our vows with me' sounds a little awkward, don't ya think? Besides...I want it to mean more than that. I don't think we really knew what we were doing the first time around. I think we looked at getting married as a way to solve all our problems without actually solving anything. It's different now. We have a chance to start our lives over, and I want to do it right. I want to look at this as a new beginning."

Caleb swallowed hard. "I want that too." He almost hated to ask, but he had to. "But what about Sally? What's she gonna think? She's already on the outside that way. I don't want to make her feel more left out."

"Oh, she doesn't feel left out." Aldo chuckled. "You can trust me on that. When I asked her about it, she said she was pretty clear on the fact that this is her show now and we're just adjuncts."

"Good to know. So how did this come about? You went and got her permission to ask me; is that what you're saying? Or was this whole thing her idea?"

"Oh, fuck you. No, it was my idea, okay? Now are you going to marry me or not?"

Caleb grinned. "'Cause that's so romantic?" He stepped in close and pressed his lips to Aldo's. "Yes, idiot. Of course. I'll marry you, as many times as you want. Just so long as we don't have to get divorced in between, because I don't want to let you get away for a minute."

"That seems reasonable enough," Aldo agreed, letting go of Caleb's hands so he could wrap his arms around him. "I think we have a deal."

"Good," Caleb said as he rested his forehead against Aldo's. "Because I love you too. But you're wearing too many clothes for me to show you how much. So let's go home and get naked while we can still do stuff like that whenever we want to."

"Now who's being romantic? I hate to break it to you, but a blowjob and love are not the same thing."

Caleb couldn't keep from laughing as they turned for home. "Really? You don't think so? Well, obviously some things do change then, because I'm pretty sure there was a time you used to think they were."

They were both still chuckling when they got back to the cabin. Sally glanced up at them from her place on the couch, where she was watching a live broadcast of the Rose Bowl Parade. She took one look at the two of them and smiled. "Congratulations. From the looks on your faces, I assume I'll need to shop for a 'best person's dress' sometime in the near future."

"And you're sure you're okay with that?" Caleb asked as the two men joined her on the couch—one on either side of her. Caleb tugged at her shoulders until she was leaning against him.

"Of course." She shifted around obligingly, moving her feet from the coffee table and resting them in Aldo's lap.

She prodded him with her foot. "Didn't you tell him what I said?" she asked.

Aldo shrugged. "I told him. I guess he needed to hear it from you."

"I just didn't want you to feel like we were taking you for granted."

Sally shook her head. "Oh, believe me, I don't. I know how crucial I am to this little family of ours, and I wouldn't have it any other way. Maybe someday I'll be able to marry the both of you and that would be wonderful but, for now, as long as I can list you both as my son's daddies on his birth certificate, I'm happy." As she spoke, she let her hand glide over her pregnant belly.

Her son. Caleb followed the motion of Sally's hand, mesmerized, amazed, grateful. Here was another change, Caleb reflected as he bent to kiss her cheek. A really big one. Another nail in the coffin of Aldo's "nothing changes" mantra, not that he felt any inclination to point that out. Besides, it was a new year, wasn't it? Maybe he should make that his resolution: no more pointless arguing with Aldo.

"Davis Evans Mosier-Nash," Aldo repeated as he massaged Sally's feet. "It's a good name."

"I think so too," Sally agreed, smiling at him.

"And I'm glad to see you're starting him off right," Aldo said, nodding at the screen. "I assume we'll be watching the game later as well? Maybe in the future we could make a new tradition. We could drive down to SoCal and watch the game live because *someone* has been complaining about the cold again." He eyed Caleb as he said it, derailing all his earlier, nonargumentative intentions.

"SoCal is fine," Caleb said. "But I'd rather go to the beach when we're down there. Besides I'm pretty sure any son of mine is gonna prefer surfing to football."

Aldo rolled his eyes. "Oh, is that so? Well, I hate to break it to you, Kay, but *my* son is going to be more of a team player than that. That's why he's going to prefer watching football with his old man."

Caleb grinned. "Hey, at least you got the *old* part right, but as for the rest..."

"Listen to the two of you." Sally glared at them both with mock sternness. "What did I just get through saying? He's *our* son, and you know what that means, don't you? It means he's going to have a mind of his own. Who knows what he'll decide to do?"

Aldo nodded. "You're right. And who cares anyway? As long as he finds something that makes him happy, that's all that matters."

"And finds a way to keep it," Caleb added. "Because I think that's the hard part."

"Not so hard," Aldo said as he turned his head to meet Caleb's gaze. He stretched his arm along the back of the couch to clasp Caleb's hand. "Once you find the right fit, once you figure out what's really important, it's not so hard at all."

About PG Forte

PG Forte inhabits a world only slightly less strange than the ones she creates. Filled with serendipity, coincidence, love at first sight and dreams come true…it also bears an uncanny resemblance to Berkeley, California.

She wrote her first serialized story when she was still in her teens. The sexy, ongoing adventure tales were very popular at her oh-so-proper, all girls, Catholic High School, where they helped to liven up otherwise dull classes.

Even if her teachers didn't always think so.

Originally a Jersey girl, PG now resides with her family on the extreme left coast where she writes rule bending, genre blending romance and paranormal stories.

When she's not pestering her husband to help her research scenes for upcoming books or being amused by her vastly entertaining children, she can usually be found serving the needs and whims of her characters...and her cats.

It's a difficult job, but someone's got to do it.

Links to reach PG Forte:

www.PGForte.com
Facebook.com/AuthorPGForte
Twitter.com/PGForte

www.ingramcontent.com/pod-product-compliance
Lightning Source LLC
Chambersburg PA
CBHW051510170626
46811CB00002B/730